D1369745

OTHER BOOKS BY EDWARD SKLEPOWICH

Liquid Desires

Farewell to the Flesh

Death in a Serene City

EDWARD SKLEPOWICH

Black Bridge

A MYSTERY OF VENICE

SCRIBNER

New York   London   Toronto   Sydney   Tokyo   Singapore

SCRIBNER
1230 Avenue of the Americas
New York, NY 10020

Manufactured in the United States of America
1 3 5 7 9 10 8 6 4 2

LIBRARY OF CONGRESS CATALOGING-IN-PUBLICATION DATA
Sklepowich, Edward.
Black bridge: a mystery of Venice/Edward Sklepowich.
p. cm.
I. Title.
PS3569.K574B58   1995
813'.54—dc20
94–40206
CIP

ISBN 0-684-81520-6

FOR MY FATHER,

FROM HIS "FAVORITE SON."

BLACK BRIDGE

All along the Grand Canal, repeated in the distance by all the boats, flowed the melody of transient pleasure.

Gabriele d'Annunzio, Fire

Belladonna

In the months afterward, whenever Urbino Macintyre looked back over the events that brought the Contessa da Capo-Zendrini so close to death, he told himself that they began one afternoon in late October at Caffè Florian.

Nothing in their immediate environment suggested the impending tragedy, however. For one thing, the Contessa was most attractively clinging to summer. Her dress was sheer, a pattern of marigolds on a wine-dark background. And she was full of life at the time, almost irritatingly so to someone like himself who had been in a bit of a funk for several weeks.

The Chinese salon, where the two friends had ensconced themselves at their accustomed table by the window, was a red-and-gold Whistler palette this afternoon. The filtered sun from Piazza San Marco, the bronze *amorini* spilling their buttery light, the Rosolio glasses with cocoa and cherry, the maroon banquettes, the gilded strips of wood and burnished parquet floor, the pattern of the Contessa's dress—even Urbino's sherry and the first-flush jasmine in the Contessa's teacup—contributed to the painterly effect.

"Go, then," the Contessa said with a barely audible sigh, "but why you think you must slap mud all over your still obscenely young body is beyond me. Your little flare-up is over, isn't it?"

"But I feel twinges."

"Twinges!" Scorn edged the Contessa's voice. "I call it hypochondria. Oh, I'm not disputing that you were indisposed with that grotesque toe of yours. I saw it, don't forget. The sight will be with me for a long time to come. But if you're really living in fear of another flare-up you shouldn't be drinking alcohol. You should be looking after yourself better—and by that I don't mean dipping yourself in mud and being maudlin about yourself. Didn't Byron swim the Hellespont and all the way from the Lido to the far end of the Grand Canal? And he had a clubfoot!"

"I don't think you understand, Barbara."

He didn't like the petulant note in his own voice. It seemed to be there more and more these days.

"Oh, but I do, my dear. You're afraid you're sliding into the most awkward age of all—the so-called middle years. You're afraid it's farewell to your youth. And, yes—admit it—you're afraid it's your first personally designed little *memento mori*. Am I right, *caro*?"

The Contessa definitely was but he didn't feel like giving her any satisfaction by saying so.

"Such a Victorian ailment," she went on. "Almost a period picture: The men indisposed with gout and the women in a vaporish swoon. I've been reading up on your indisposition. Alexander the Great, Michelangelo, Henry the Eighth—no, forget him, I suppose, although he's given me an idea for your Christmas gift: One of those stools he rested his gouty foot on. Don't get all ruffled! I think you're losing your sense of humor and when that goes, my friend—"

She shook her head forebodingly. Urbino pretended an interest in the game of chess a German couple was playing at a nearby table on a small, portable chessboard.

"But please!" the Contessa continued, unable to restrain herself from giving him more advice. "Don't become one of those desperate souls who tries to keep nature at bay. Monkey glands! Calf embryos! And those liver injections Harriet gets at that Dracula Institute up in Hungary!" The Contessa shook her stylishly coifed honey blond head slowly. She was referring to Harriet Kolb, her live-in social secretary who was obsessed with quack cures and psychics. "It may all begin with mud!"

"I seem to remember that you indulged yourself in a whole week's worth of mud at Montecatini two years ago."

"Oh, that!" The Contessa languidly waved a beringed hand in

the air. "That *fango* was for my face," she said, using the Italian word as if it described something more evolved than the mud of the Montecatini spa near Florence.

She lifted the selfsame face up as if inviting Urbino to inspect the wonders of *fango* applied where it should be. She had never divulged the actual, incriminating number of her age, but, according to Urbino's computations, it had to be close to two decades more than his own rapidly approaching four. It was an attractive face which fine bone structure, good genes, and the judicious application of makeup—and perhaps even *fango*—made look at least ten years younger.

"At any rate, Urbino, Montecatini was more for Oriana's sake. She needed someone to confide in during the few moments she wasn't with her Berliner. Come to think of it, *he* had the gout. In his sixties though," she added with a smile. "Speaking of Oriana, you've been very remiss about her new friend, especially since he's an American."

This concern for Oriana's love affairs was a new note for the Contessa to strike.

"Why bother? For one thing, I don't particularly like Flint, whether he's an American or not."

"But he's so handsome, wouldn't you say?"

"Handsome, yes, and very clever as well. He's taking full advantage of Oriana."

"No one could ever do that. She's a real tiger!"

A leopard would have been a more appropriate animal, Urbino thought, given some of her outfits, but he said instead: "At any rate, it'll soon be over. It's already gone on much longer than any of her other affairs."

"That's just it, *caro*. It's been going on for months and months, and I'm quite sure it's not an affair."

"What do you call it when she's married to Filippo?"

"I call it quite simply love!"

Urbino now knew he could no longer ignore the change in his usually predictable Contessa.

"Love! You must be kidding."

"I don't believe I could be accused of ever 'kidding' in my life, certainly never about love, Urbino dear."

He looked out into Piazza San Marco. What Napoleon had called the finest drawing room of Europe had regained some of its sedateness after the insanity of high season. The hordes of boisterous tourists had departed. In their place were people who gazed instead of gaped and who negotiated the square and arcades with almost an air of indolence.

His favorite months in Venice were upon them, and he had been looking forward to consoling, restorative hours of the Contessa's company. Long strings of mornings at the museums, afternoons like these at Florian's, day trips to Torcello and Florence, dinners at their favorite restaurants, concerts and operas at the Teatro del Ridotto and the Teatro La Fenice, and intimate evenings in the Ca' da Capo-Zendrini.

But he had been deluding himself. Her comments about Oriana's newest lover indicated just how little she was herself these days. He believed he knew why. Her next comment proved him right.

"You realize, *caro*, don't you, that you have to be back from Abano in time for Bobo's opening night?"

Bobo—or the Barone Roberto Casarotto-Re, a longtime friend of the Contessa and her deceased husband—was coming to town to perform in his one-man show on the controversial writer Gabriele d'Annunzio. Although Urbino had never met him, he had heard about him—all too much, in fact, during the past few months.

The Contessa lowered her eyes to her dress and removed a nonexistent speck from its background.

"Oh, you'll just love Bobo! He's practically devoted his entire life to the ugly little man."

The Barone himself, however, was in no way an "ugly little man." If the Contessa's descriptions had made Urbino think she might be exaggerating, two photographs had quickly disillusioned him. One showed a handsome, vigorous man in tennis whites, who, to Urbino's amazement, the Contessa said was sixty-five. The other was his publicity photo. Taken ten years ago, it revealed how little the noble, leonine Barone had changed.

"I wouldn't miss the opening of the Barone's impersonation for anything!"

"Bobo gives a performance, Urbino. *Pomegranate* is a play based on his own script, as you well know. We're not going to have any problems, are we? 'Problems' because you're too preoccupied with your toe to be able to enjoy yourself and—and to let others do the same!"

She sighed and reached out to touch his hand.

"I worry about you," she went on. "I couldn't worry more if I were your—your—" She searched for the right relationship, then abandoned the attempt. "Oh, I've seen how you look at people enjoying themselves. Like that sweet couple sitting there on the steps." She cast an indulgent glance at a boy and girl snacking on cheese and bread, a sight which on previous occasions would have provoked her. "You're envious! Envious of how they seem to be able to enjoy so much with so little, to possess the whole of Venice from their humble little perch. No, it doesn't take much, does it? There's a great deal of consolation in that," she said as if she weren't one of the wealthiest women in Venice.

She was silent for a few moments as she gazed out at the couple from her own far from humble perch, then, with the manner of rousing herself from a dream: "So drive any silly notions about being ill out of your head. You've got so much to look forward to. We *both* have!"

The Contessa's face was glowing, and it wasn't artifice or the warm colors and golden light of Florian's.

"In addition to Bobo, *caro*, there's this lovely weather, the end of the tourist season, and my bridge of boats. Of course, though, that's on a more somber note."

The bridge of boats was a pontoon bridge across the lagoon to the cemetery island of San Michele on November 2, the Day of All

Souls. She referred to it proprietarily as "hers" because she was reviving—and underwriting—the solemn Venetian tradition.

She spread orange marmalade over a piece of toasted scone and added a generous dollop of whipped cream. She held the scone out to Urbino.

"For you, *caro*. To soothe you. It won't do you any harm."

She prepared another piece for herself, an almost imperceptible frown wrinkling her brow, then said: "You'll be your usual sweet self to Bobo, won't you? He was one of Alvise's best friends. Ever since Rosa died, life seems to have lost a lot of its flavor for him. I'm happy that he's finally having the success he deserves."

"Bobo! Isn't that a rather juvenile name for a man his age?"

"It's endearing! It captures a *je ne sais quoi* about him. Oh, you'll see, *caro*! She then wove an anecdote about the man astride his horse in the Campania. "Just like Colleoni!" she enthused. She was referring to the imposing equestrian statue of the *condottiere* in front of San Zanipolo, which at this time of the day was bathed in tones as golden as the words she was lavishing on Bobo.

The more the Contessa waxed, the more Urbino waned. All he could think of was what a disaster on horseback he had always been. And surely the Barone, despite his greater years, had never been cursed with an ailment as embarrassing as gout!

Urbino prepared himself for a long, uncomfortable session when the Contessa no sooner finished the one anecdote than she began another, this one about the Barone's brave rescue of his brother-in-law from the sea at Taormina.

He was therefore relieved when a woman in her late thirties came over to their table. It was Harriet Kolb, the Contessa's social secretary, a thin, unprepossessing woman with a receding chin. Her brown hair had recently been styled in stiff waves and she had added an uncharacteristic bit of flair to her usual brown cardigan and navy skirt in the form of a designer scarf and gold sea horse pin.

"Would you look through these pieces on the Barone for the *Gazzettino*, Barbara?"

She handed her a manila folder. The Contessa took out several sheets and a black-and-white photograph. She gave Urbino the photograph.

It was of the Barone Bobo at Gabriele d'Annunzio's home at Lago di Garda. He stood next to a cradle-coffin D'Annunzio had been fond of reclining in. The pose was self-conscious but it didn't detract from the Barone's striking looks.

"*Bellissimo!*" Harriet said and made a sound somewhere between a giggle and a whinny. "I can't wait to meet him. By the way, Urbino, you're not looking as fit as usual, if you don't mind my saying so. That gout attack a few weeks ago might have taken more out of you than you realize. Are you avoiding nightshade?"

"I hope so. Isn't that a poison—belladonna?"

Harriet gave a shrill, high laugh.

"Oh, avoid that at all costs! But only some nightshades are poisonous. Not potatoes, eggplants, peppers, and tomatoes, although they might as well be for people like you and me! I stopped eating them in July. My joints are much better now."

She flexed one of her elbows to demonstrate the results of avoiding the dreaded nightshade.

"My elbows used to be as pointed as daggers. They felt as if they—"

As Harriet ran on about nightshades and her joints, Urbino wondered how the woman could possibly be without one single eccentricity when it came to her work, as the Contessa claimed. The Contessa waited with a tolerant smile for her to finish, then handed back the folder.

"I'd better get these over to the *Gazzettino* then," Harriet said. "There are some letters on the desk for you to sign. I'll post them in the morning."

"I think Harriet has a crush on Bobo, don't you?" the Contessa said when the woman had left. "How you can be so impervious to his charm is beyond me!"

"But I haven't met him yet!"

"Neither has Harriet, and see how smitten she is! Oh, you're blind, Urbino! First with Oriana, and now Harriet."

"Blind?"

"Blind to the mischievous little boy with arrows!" She looked fondly over at one of the bronze *amorini*. "You're missing so much!"

Her eyes were shining. If she was this way now, whatever would she be like when the Barone made his descent on Venice in all his talent and vigor?

"Oh, we're all going to have such a wonderful time together, *caro!*" the Contessa exclaimed. "Just you wait and see!"

Urbino had his doubts.

PART ONE

Murder on the Rialto

1

Wrapped in a canvas sheet and covered in one-hundred-and-ten-degree mud, Urbino lay on a gurney in one of the therapy rooms in Abano Terme. He felt as if he were in a secret room of the Marquis de Sade's château, surrounded as he was by antiseptic tiles, grotesque protrusions of spigots and hoses, and an ominous gaping drain in the floor. Only his face, chest, and right arm were free. The therapist had said he would be back in twenty minutes.

Urbino hoped so. Only five minutes had passed and he already felt like calling for help. Thank God for his free hand, which was intended to give the guests—never were they "patients"—the sense that they weren't completely restrained. He raised it to wipe beads of sweat from his forehead and tried to think pleasant thoughts.

He wasn't successful. How could he be, wrapped up like a corpse in a morgue? He was also dead tired, having tossed and turned for two nights in his overheated room, where a sulfurous odor had seeped under the door—the same sulfurous odor that was all around him now and that seemed to suffuse everything and everyone at the spa.

Why not just admit it? He had made a mistake. It would have been better to have checked into the Grand Hotel des Bains on the Lido or the Hassler Villa Medici down in Rome for a complete change of scene, but he'd stick things through for two more days. The Contessa wasn't expecting him back until then. In fact, she might not be that pleased to see him, occupied as she was with the Barone Bobo.

Two hours later, after a spell of sweating induced by the mud therapy that was supposed to "rid his body of its toxicity,"

23

Urbino had a massage, then went to the pool. As he finished his last lap, he looked up to see Marco Zeoli's long, thin face, etched as it always seemed to be with fatigue. The assistant medical director of the spa held out a towel.

Zeoli was doing everything to make Urbino's stay as enjoyable as possible, in the hope that he would praise the spa to the Anglo-American community in Venice. If all went well for him, Zeoli, only forty-one, would soon be made chief medical director. He had been there for almost fifteen years, commuting the twenty-five miles from Venice, where he lived with his widowed mother.

"You seem in fine form, Urbino."

Zeoli's cold, exact voice suited his severe look. He had always reminded Urbino of a figure out of a Goya painting. It was amusing, if not also a little disconcerting, that a man in his position didn't emanate more of an air of healthiness, unless it was to be found in the ever so faint whiff of the spa's salubrious sulfur that clung to his sallow skin.

"Not everyone comes here because of a problem, and yours is quite minor as far as these things go," Zeoli quickly added. His professional eye made a quick examination of Urbino's right big toe as Urbino dried himself off. "Quite a few come just for rest and recreation—from as far away as England and Germany. That man and woman over there"—he indicated a late-middle-aged couple with round, healthy faces and reddish hair—"come all the way from Finland every year, and they're in the best of health. Remember that Abano's mud and thermal waters have drawn people since the time of the Romans. Maybe you can come back and work on your newest book. Our library is the best in Abano. If you have any problems or suggestions, let me know. Good day."

Zeoli left.

As he sat in a poolside chair, Urbino thought about what Zeoli had said about the Romans and smiled to himself. The men and women in their white robes, in fact, did look a little like toga-clad Romans, especially an overweight, homely man taking off his robe at the other end of the pool. With his round, completely bald head and pendulous lower lip, he resembled a corrupt senator from the time of the Caesars. It was only his unmistakable aura of sorrow and preoccupation that softened the edges of the image. He caught Urbino staring at him and frowned.

Urbino turned his attention to *Fire*, D'Annunzio's novel about Venice, a fictionalized account of his affair with the actress Eleonora Duse. The hero was delivering a paeon to Venice at the Doges' Palace while his aging mistress gazed adoringly at him from the crowd. The scene was filled with passion and bombast, poetry and prophecy, which managed to be somehow both inspiring and ridiculous at the same time.

Despite all D'Annunzio's excesses, you could easily be drawn in, as Urbino was now. This was D'Annunzio's power, a power that the unattractive little man had exerted not only on the page but in the bedroom. All this made Urbino apprehensive about the Barone Casarotto-Re, who supposedly resurrected D'Annunzio's spirit, though obviously not his homely flesh.

"Excuse me, Signor Macintyre." It was the pool attendant with a portable phone. "You have a call."

"Urbino!" Urgency charged the Contessa's voice. "I hate to bother you in the midst of your mud"—her light laugh sounded strained—"but there's a problem. Everything is at sixes and sevens! Bobo is being threatened! You have to come back to Venice immediately and do something!"

"What's happened?"

"Have some sense! I can't go into detail over the phone. Come back to Venice. I'm counting on you."

Urbino sighed. Suddenly, illogically, he didn't want to leave Abano. What was the Contessa pulling him back to? And what did it have to do with the Barone Bobo?

"All right, Barbara. The train will get me in at seven-fifteen. Have Milo meet me with the boat."

Urbino could feel the Contessa's relief over the line.

"I'll make up for dragging you out of the mud like this, *caro*. I promise."

When Urbino joined the Contessa in her *salotto blu* at the Ca' da Capo-Zendrini, her face was becomingly flushed and the bridge of her nose was slightly sunburned, something she had never allowed to happen for as long as he had known her.

"Bobo is resting at the Gritti. He's been through so much in the past six hours, poor dear—and so have I! There we were at the Cipriani, having such a pleasant time with Oriana and John! Little did we know what was brewing for poor Bobo!" She sighed and shook her head, displaying brighter highlights in her hair than three days ago. "Would you make me another g-and-t?"

The Contessa's request and the empty glass she held out to him were the most vivid evidence she could have given of her strange state, for tea, mineral water, and wine were her accustomed drinks. Gin-and-tonic was for only special and not always the most auspicious occasions. Urbino knew very well that he should avoid alcohol because of his condition, but he felt he needed a drink to get him through whatever lay ahead. He fixed two gin-and-tonics. The Contessa took a sip of hers and narrowed her gray eyes as if she had just had a dose of medicine.

"Some envious, mean-spirited person is trying to undermine Bobo's success."

She stared at Urbino for a few moments as if she suspected him of the deed.

"You mentioned that he received threats."

"Not directly—not yet anyway. One was put in the *bocca di leone* at the Doges' Palace."

Bocche dei leoni—or Lion's Mouths—had been placed through-out the city during the iron rule of the notorious Council of Ten. Denunciations against citizens had been deposited in the marble boxes sculpted with lions and had often led to inquisitions, torture, and death. The ones at the Doges' Palace were among the few still left in the city, these days usually crammed with gum and cigarette wrappers.

"Here's a copy."

She unfolded a white sheet the size of typewriter paper and handed it to him. Several sentences were printed in Italian in block letters in the middle of the sheet:

THE BARONE ROBERTO CASAROTTO-RE IS AS IMMORAL AS GABRIELE D'ANNUNZIO, THE MAN HE USES FOR A MASK. THE ONLY DIFFERENCE IS THAT D'ANNUNZIO IS DEAD AND CAN NO LONGER HARM ANYONE. THE TRUTH WILL COME OUT.

"The original was on red paper, folded, and slipped into the *bocca*," the Contessa explained. "The director of the Doges' Palace called the police. The *Gazzettino* got the same sheet in the mail with fifty thousand lire. The manager assumed it was meant to cover the cost of an ad but he didn't print it. He called the Questura, too."

"What does the Barone say about it?" Urbino asked, handing the sheet back.

"Bobo is being brave, the dear man! He's trying to brush it off as a prank but he's upset. Who wouldn't be?"

"And he has no idea what it's about?"

"Absolutely none! How could he? There's nothing in those things but envy and mean-spiritedness! He's one of the most upright people I know. I have a nose for falseness"—she had a fine patrician nose which did, indeed, seem made for scenting out the undesirable—"and Bobo is as true as they come. He's being done an abominable injustice and I want you to get to the bottom of it. You will, won't you?"

"What did he say about that?"

"Oh, he's so self-sacrificing! He said there isn't any need for you—or anyone—to do anything, it will all blow over, but I don't believe him. What I *mean*," she clarified, "is that, yes, I believe him, but he's wrong. It isn't over. He's trying to minimize things for my sake. But with you, he might tell the truth. I mean," she repeated with a touch of impatience, "that with you he'll be more inclined to say how he really feels about this beastly situation!"

"Ah, but you're wrong, Barbara dear," a deep male voice said in British-inflected English from the doorway. "What I tell you and what I tell others will always be the same. On that you can rest secure. You must be Barbara's dear friend Urbino. It's a pleasure to meet you."

The Barone Casarotto-Re strode over and looked down at Urbino from his six-plus feet of height. He grasped Urbino's hand and gave it a firm shake.

Everything about the Barone Roberto Casarotto-Re seemed to shout with vigor—his clear dark eyes, his olive skin, his sinewy figure, even his white hair, which had receded but not noticeably thinned. The Barone's teeth, however, were perhaps too white and too regular to be real.

Before Urbino had time to realize what the Contessa was doing, she spirited away her gin-and-tonic to the drink table and rang for Lucia to bring in the tea tray. The Barone went over and kissed her cheek.

"You and Urbino should get to know each other a little before you settle down to talk about serious things, Bobo. Everything is going to be fine. Don't you worry."

The Contessa gave his arm a reassuring, lingering pat.

"But I'm not worrying, Barbara dear, not in the slightest. I apologize for Barbara pulling you back to Venice. She's very naughty sometimes, but we have to forgive her, because we know how devoted she is." His long upper lip curled into a smile. "And I know how particularly devoted she is to you, Urbino, if I may call you that. A lovely name—and a lovely city with its associations with Raphael. Please call me Bobo. Barbara has told me all about you. Not all your secrets—ha, ha! Perhaps they will come with time. No, not everything, but enough to whet my appetite. Ah, yes, and she's told me about your problem," the Barone continued, seemingly filled with illimitable energy and enthusiasm. "I mean your problem *down there*, my friend."

He pointed a long, well-manicured finger at Urbino's Gucci-shod foot. The Contessa had a fixed smile on her face and didn't meet Urbino's eyes.

"A bit young for that, but I'm far from an expert on matters medical. Never been indisposed the same way myself. Hardly been ill a day in my life. One of these days I'm going to have to pay for it."

"Let it be ever so distant, Bobo."

"You should take better care of yourself," the Barone went on. "For example, that drink you have there. The culprit alcohol is lurking in it, just waiting to go down to that toe of yours and do its wicked little damage."

Fortunately, the Barone abruptly changed the topic when the Contessa joked about Urbino being smothered in Abano mud. He threw himself into a description of his tennis match that morning at the Cipriani Hotel with the Contessa, Oriana, and John Flint, her most recent *innamorato*. He urged the need for exercise on Urbino, squinting at him with his dark brown eyes as if he could see through Urbino's Ermenegildo Zegna suit to the supposedly exercise-starved flesh beneath.

His monologue wasn't interrupted by Lucia bringing in the tea things. Urbino wondered how long the man could go on like

29

this until he remembered that he had a one-man show that lasted for more than an hour. The Contessa prepared the tea but kept shooting nervous glances at the two men. Relief from the Barone's flow came only with his first sip of tea, but even this relief was momentary.

"You make the most delicious tea. How do you ever manage it?"

"Mother always said that you should recite the Miserere. When you finish, the tea is done to perfection."

"And so your tea always is, my dear. Your mother was a wise and—from her photograph—a beautiful woman."

The Barone put down his cup and reached into his jacket pocket to take out a chased-gold cigarette case. The Contessa, who preferred no one to smoke in the *salotto*—or, in fact, anywhere near her—seemed far from demurring when the Barone lit a Gauloise with a gold lighter. The Contessa's eyes wavered for a moment in Urbino's direction.

Before the Barone could launch into another monologue, Urbino said: "Excuse me, Barone, but—"

"Bobo," the Barone said. He exhaled a curling stream of smoke in the direction of the Contessa's collection of ceramic animals.

"What I was going to say, Bobo"—the name didn't come easily to Urbino's lips—"is that you don't seem as upset as I would be. That seems strange."

"Urbino!"

"Not at all, Barbara dear. He's right—and he's right to say it. I admire honesty. The poor boy has been dragged back from his needed therapy and I'm not being appreciative of his sacrifice. But you see, Urbino, I don't want to blow this out of proportion. I hate to see Barbara all wrought up. She's afraid I'll—what did you call it, my dear?—'dry up.' Perhaps it's best to let this business alone."

"Let it alone? *I* wouldn't want something like this left alone if I were being threatened. I'd want to find out if anyone meant me any harm. Of course, people who are serious about doing harm seldom give warning. They just strike out. This might only be a version of a poison-pen letter, but nonetheless there is a threat." Urbino went over to the table and picked up the sheet. "What does it say? 'The only difference is that D'Annunzio is dead.' "

"It gives me a chill, Bobo! You *must* take it seriously."

"Why would anyone want to harm me? No, Barbara, it's D'Annunzio this crackpot wants to harm. He has enemies even today. This could be literary criticism masquerading as an attack on my reputation! I can endure it! I have nothing to hide and just as little to fear."

"What do the police say?" Urbino asked.

"Oh, they'll send someone to the Doges' Palace and to the *Gazzettino*, I suppose," the Barone said in an offhand manner. "The Commissario wasn't much concerned."

"If *you* don't make it seem as if you care, Bobo, the police aren't going to try very hard. Urbino is good at these things. He can ask around and maybe get some answers the police wouldn't get. You know how Italians clam up when the police come along."

"I'm afraid he'd be wasting his fine talents on this silly affair." He shook his head dismissively. "And who knows? If you start poking around, Urbino, we could be playing right into the hands of this prankster."

"I think there's more danger in doing nothing. Have you ever had any problem like this before?"

"Never!" He gave a laugh that seemed to be more nervousness than humor. "Oh, there once was some trouble during a performance in Milan. Some self-styled anti-fascists and women modeling themselves after your American feminists, Urbino. There were posters—'BURN D'ANNUNZIO,' 'D'ANNUNZIO: MAN AGAINST PEACE, MAN AGAINST WOMEN.' Got in the newspapers. But it came to nothing in the end. This is just more of the same thing."

"But if it *isn't*, Bobo! Urbino is very discreet. I couldn't bear it if there was even the slimmest possibility that you were in danger from some crackpot—or even embarrassed or inconvenienced."

A look of irritation passed over the Barone's face. Urbino sensed that he usually got his way and wasn't taking this defeat well. The Barone got up and went over to the Contessa and bent down to plant a kiss on her forehead.

"As you wish, for your own dear sake. Do what you can, Urbino, but be as discreet as Barbara says you are. And now, for the rest of our evening, let's talk about more pleasant things. Tell me about that little palazzo you inherited from your mother, Urbino, and about your Venetian biographies. By the way, do you think you'll ever write one on D'Annunzio? Perhaps I could be of help if you do. For example, did you know that when he was living in the Casetta Rossa on the Grand Canal—"

The Barone then shared some of his hero's amorous adventures. The Contessa listened with such rapt attention that her tea grew cold. The conversation never got around to Urbino's Palazzo Uccello or his Venetian Lives.

The next morning Urbino was in the Sala della Bussola at the Doges' Palace. It was the waiting room of the Council of Ten, the much-feared intelligence agency of the former Venetian Republic. Only a handful of tourists were in the room, eager to move on to the more sensational parts of the Doges' Palace. Few of them noted an unassuming object built into one of the walls. This was the "lion's mouth" into which someone had dropped a threat against the Barone Bobo. Once you slipped something into the *bocca* through the slot on the other side of the wall, it couldn't be retrieved except from this room. The metal lid of the *bocca*, which in the old days had been kept locked, was open.

Urbino reached over the velvet cords and put his hand into the stone-lined box within. It was empty.

"You're not supposed to do that, Signore."

Urbino turned and saw a young man with an official tag on his pocket.

"Sorry. Perhaps you could help me. Do you know anything about the red sheet of paper found in the *bocca di leone* yesterday? I'm making inquiries on behalf of the Contessa da Capo-Zendrini. It was her friend whose name was on the sheet."

Urbino slipped him two ten-lira notes.

"The Barone something-or-other," the guard said. "I found it about eleven in the morning. I turned it over to the director."

"Did you see anyone put anything into the *bocca* yesterday— or maybe the day before?"

There was a canvas chair on the other side of the doorway in the next room where the guard usually sat to give him a view of both rooms.

"Had to be yesterday. We check every day. No, I didn't see anyone do it—but it could have been slipped through the slot on this side." They went into the hallway. The guard pointed to a stone slab with a slot that had indecipherable words chiseled in Italian beneath. "I don't go into the hall often."

"Did you notice anyone acting suspiciously?"

"Well, there was a man about sixty. He was studying the ceiling for a long time. One of the first to come in when we opened." The guard glanced up at the wooden ceiling with its painting of St. Mark surrounded by angels. "Usually people move through this room fast. Not much to see except the *bocca*. The good stuff was taken away by Napoleon. A lot's in the Louvre. That's why I thought it was odd for him to be studying the ceiling since it's only a copy of the Veronese."

"Could you describe him a bit more?"

"Dressed in good clothes and shoes. I always notice the shoes." He glanced down at Urbino's Gucci loafers. "But I didn't get much of a chance to see his face. He had a fedora pulled

Edward Sklepowich

down low. Had to tilt his head way back to get a good look at the ceiling. I wondered why he didn't just take it off. Italian—or someone who spoke the language as well as one. He asked me what time it was. Seemed to be waiting for someone and then all of a sudden he slipped away. But it didn't have to be him. Anyone could have slipped the paper into the *bocca*."

Urbino left the Doges' Palace and went across the Piazza to the offices of the *Gazzettino* by the Clock Tower and asked to speak with the manager.

"Yes, we received a similar sheet in yesterday's mail," the bespectacled man said, looking at the copy Urbino had handed him. "Fifty thousand lire were enclosed, but no note of explanation. Of course we didn't print it."

"Do you still have the envelope?"

"The police have the envelope and the note. We called them right away. It seemed like a prank but we have to protect people like the Barone Casarotto-Re."

"Or any ordinary citizen, as well, I'm sure. What was the postmark on the envelope?"

"Venice. The main post office behind Piazza San Marco. It even arrived the next day. Quite an achievement for Venice or for anywhere in Italy."

Urbino walked the short distance to Harry's Bar. The small, unpretentious room was crowded and smoke-filled, mainly with tourists with obligatory Bellinis. He sat at the bar, ordered a Campari soda, and looked through that day's *Gazzettino*. There was no mention of the threats against the Barone Casarotto-Re, but there was an article about Bobo's upcoming show at the Teatro del Ridotto:

> The Barone Roberto Casarotto-Re, actor, playwright, and author, will appear in his one-man show, *Pomegranate: Scenes from the Life and Writings of Gabriele d'Annunzio*, at the Teatro del Ridotto on the evenings of 22, 23, and 24 October at 8:30 P.M.

The Barone Casarotto-Re has given his show to considerable acclaim in Rome, Milan, and Paris and will take an English-language version to London and New York in the New Year.

The Barone Casarotto-Re is also the author of *I See the Sun*, a play based on the love affair between D'Annunzio and the actress Eleonora Duse. The Barone will sign copies of his plays at the Libreria Sangiorgio at four o'clock on 23 October.

Urbino had just finished the piece when someone came up behind his stool. It was Oriana Borelli.

"It *is* you, Urbino! Come over here. There's someone who would like to meet you."

Oriana dragged him over to a table under the windows where three people were sitting. One of them was John Flint, Oriana's latest distraction—or, as the Contessa saw it, the man she was in love with. He was a tall man in his mid-thirties with short blond hair, bright blue eyes, full lips, and an expression that didn't vary much between sullenness and insolence. He was perhaps the epitome of one type of masculine beauty and always seemed to be aware of it. Across from him were a dark woman and a thin young man with untidy hair. Urbino pulled over another chair and sat at the end of the table.

"Well, Urbino, I hope you'll give this young couple a few minutes of your time even if you haven't condescended to give any to poor John yet! This is Marie Quimper and Hugh Moss. John and I met them at the Palazzo Grassi exhibit. They've been eager to meet you."

Moss seemed far from eager about anything except the martini that he lifted to his lips. But then Urbino noticed his eyes. They were particularly sharp and assessing.

"It's a pleasure to make your acquaintance, Monsieur Macintyre," the small, dark-haired woman said timidly. She was what the French call a *belle-laide*, an ugly but somehow also attractive woman. Moss said nothing, but only nodded his head curtly.

"I like your book on Proust very much."

A bit nervously, she reached into her large leather pocketbook and took out Urbino's biography of Proust.

"Would you mind signing it? 'To Marie.'"

When he opened the book to sign it, a small slip of white paper fluttered to the floor. It was a cash register receipt. Urbino picked it up. The book had been bought that day at the Libreria Sangiorgio behind San Marco, Urbino's favorite bookstore in Venice, and where the Barone would be signing copies of his books. Hugh Moss glared at his companion, who had turned pale. Urbino put the receipt back in the book, signed it with his fountain pen, and handed it back to Quimper. Quimper, somewhat breathlessly and almost with an air of recitation, started to tell Urbino some of the things she liked about his book when Moss interrupted in a chilly, controlled voice: "Is your friend the Contessa da Capo-Zendrini here?"

"You dedicated the book to her," Marie Quimper said quickly, looking uneasily at Moss.

"No, Hugh dear," Oriana said, "Barbara isn't lurking around here somewhere! I believe she's in the company of a certain barone at the moment." She glanced playfully at Urbino. "But you'll get to meet her *and* her Barone, who's giving the show at the Teatro del Ridotto. Don't forget you're both coming to the performance and the Contessa's reception afterward—as my guests. You know, Urbino dear," she said, turning her Laura Biagiotti sunglasses back in Urbino's direction, "with Barbara so occupied these days you have even less excuse to avoid John. And to think you both come from the 'heart of Dixie'! Isn't that what you called it, John?"

Flint was from Mississippi.

"Oriana, you know how it is," Flint said in a Southern drawl. "The last thing people abroad want to see is someone from back home."

"But Urbino isn't abroad, my sweet little boy! He lives here.

And so do you! But we'll excuse him if he mends his ways. After all, the poor man has been ill enough to seek out the muds of Abano!"

Hugh Moss gave a slight start.

"Abano?" he repeated.

"Yes! Mud therapy with all those Germans! But don't try to use your indisposition as an excuse. You simply must take John under your wing. He has so many marvelous ideas." Flint was a former Milan fashion model, now an art consultant seeking wealthy clients. "Barbara has been helping him, and I'm sure Bobo will, too."

Flint had enough good sense not to look too self-satisfied.

"I hear that the Barone Casarotto-Re's show is all about someone named D'Annunzio," he said. "I'm sure you know a lot about him. Maybe you could tell us a few things so that we'll be able to follow the play better."

"D'Annunzio, darling? I thought you knew all about him," Oriana jumped in. "A writer, of course. Stories and poems about love and passion, written in a voluptuous style. If only you knew Italian well enough to appreciate it! Homely as sin, but women found him irresistible. He had affairs with a clutch of contessas, one of them went stark raving mad, and one of them was even named Barbara! There was an affair with a marchesa—the Medusa of the Great Hotels, she was called!—who lived on the Grand Canal in the Unfinished Palazzo before the Guggenheim woman bought it up. She threw mad parties with ocelots and naked boys painted gold! D'Annunzio lived in the sweet little house across the way. The Casetta Rossa. Then there was his marvelous affair with Sarah Bernhardt's rival, Eleonora Duse. She was much older than he was." She looked at Flint to be sure this point wasn't lost on him. "Hmmm, let me think. He also had affairs with rich American painters and Jewish dancers, had acid poured on his head and went bald, fought during the First World War, flew planes, bombed places—or torpedoed them, I forget which—went blind in one eye, fell from a window, or maybe he was pushed or tried to kill himself, I don't remember. He was a bit of a *fascista*, too. Mussolini made him the Prince of the Peak or the Snowy Mountain or something like that. In his twilight years he had orgies in a Wagnerian house on Lago di Garda."

She seemed to have finished but then added: "Oh, and he slept with boys and died on his way to dinner."

Oriana gave them all a bright smile, not even breathing heavily or seeming the slightest bit exhausted. Quimper looked shocked and glanced at Moss, who had a bored expression. Flint had struck a pose somewhere between bemusement and admiration.

"You've said it all, Oriana," Urbino said. "It certainly will be interesting to see how the Barone will be able to transform himself into a short, ugly, bald man!"

There was an unpleasant little twist to Moss's thin lips, quickly erased.

"No problem there, Urbino dear. We all want to be deceived! And Bobo is such a master that he gives his performance with hardly any makeup! I was completely carried away in Milan, and so was every other woman in the audience."

A few minutes later Oriana and her entourage got up and left. Urbino ordered another drink and sat thinking about the man who had shown an interest in the ceiling of the Sala della Bussola.

The guard's description was general enough to be any number of sixty-year-old men, yet specific enough to call to mind the Barone. But if he had been at the Doges' Palace, why hadn't he mentioned it last night? The most obvious answer was that he had slipped the threat into the *bocca* himself. He had been reluctant to have Urbino investigate and had agreed only when the Contessa had been so insistent. Was this whole business just the Barone's attempt to draw attention to his production? The threat sent to the *Gazzettino* made this seem even more probable. But if he had been trying to get publicity, he would have been more eager for it all to come out, not reluctant to have the situation looked into—as long as an investigation didn't reveal that he had made the threats himself.

What kind of game might the Barone be playing? Surely the man was being devious. Urbino was going to have to be wary—not only of the Barone but of his own responses as well.

Urbino called the Contessa and asked her and the Barone to be at Caffè Florian at five that afternoon.

A cloud of cigarette smoke hung over the Contessa's head and dipped toward the tray of petits fours on the mahogany serving table in the Chinese salon. The Barone Bobo held a Gauloise between his long fingers. The Contessa's eyelids were slightly closed against the smoke, giving them an oriental look that went with the salon.

"Here's our sleuth," the Barone said with a show of impressive teeth as Urbino came over to their table. "You look far less rumpled than your compatriots of the same profession, I must say."

"It's not his profession, Bobo dear. Like all amateurs he does it for the pure love of it. It's an inclination."

"That's not quite true either. I don't usually seek cases out."

"They seek you! Ha, ha! Then it's *not* an avocation at all, Barbara, but a true *vocation* in the religious sense. Our Urbino hasn't chosen a life of sleuthing, but has been called to it by a higher power—in this particular case, by you and your gentle insistence."

"Urbino never needs any insistence to do the right thing," the Contessa said with a smile that tried to take in both her male companions.

"So what do you have to tell us?" the Barone asked when they were settled with their drinks—a gin-and-tonic for Urbino and a fresh pot of tea for the Contessa and the Barone Bobo. The Barone Bobo didn't impress Urbino as a tea-drinking man but he seemed willing enough to imbibe for the sake of the Contessa. He didn't refrain from smoking, however, which showed less consideration—or was it less design? Could it be possible that she hadn't made her dislike known?

After Urbino told them what he had learned at the Doges' Palace and the *Gazzettino*, there was a momentary silence. Then the Contessa, with a worried look, said: "Well, I don't know whether to be pleased or disappointed. You didn't learn much, did you?"

"But I didn't think he would," the Barone said, not without a note of satisfaction. "Don't misunderstand me, Urbino. It has nothing to do with your sleuthing abilities but with the fact that there's nothing *to* be learned from delving into this silly business. I knew that from the start. I suggest that we simply forget it."

"I wouldn't say that we didn't learn much," Urbino said. "For one thing, we know that the threat sent to the *Gazzettino* was postmarked at the main post office here. It means that whoever sent it was here or had someone mail it from here. We also have the description of the man in a fedora who spent such an unusual amount of time in the Sala della Bussola. Do you have any idea who he might be?"

"Absolutely none," the Barone said without any hesitation. "Unless it was Orlando!" he added with a laugh.

"He means his brother-in-law, Orlando Gava," the Contessa explained. "Orlando is Rosa's brother. But why would gentle Orlando do something like that, Bobo?"

"I was just trying to show how preposterous this whole thing is."

"You said the man was wearing a brown fedora," the Contessa said, reaching for a petit four. She took a bite. "You have a brown fedora, Bobo. You know what that means, don't you, Urbino? Someone is trying to impersonate him! The good clothes, the handmade shoes, the brown fedora. It's obvious! It goes along with the threats."

"It's possible," Urbino admitted.

"Don't be so enthusiastic!" the Contessa said. She reached for another petit four but pulled her hand back into her lap and sighed. "I'm sorry, Urbino. My nerves are frazzled. And I'm a bit knackered. I had too much Cabernet at the Graspo de Ua," she said, naming one of her and Urbino's favorite restaurants. "You know how quickly even a little wine goes to my head."

"To your sweet head," the Barone corrected, touching her hand. "I can see that you'll be in dreamland early tonight, leaving me to my own lonely devices. But I have a thought, Urbino!" he exclaimed with an attempt at spontaneity. "Why don't the two of us have a nightcap at the Gritti Palace about ten?"

"That would be lovely!" the Contessa answered for Urbino. "You can make it, can't you?"

Urbino said he would be there and left. Out in Piazza San Marco he tried to shake his annoyance with the Barone. He barely knew him. Although he trusted his instincts and believed in first impressions, he often made mistakes by being too sensitive, and this autumn his illness, minor though it was, had drained a lot of his reserves. He couldn't concentrate as he usually did and had a vague feeling of sadness. He had hoped the Contessa would be a big help to him but she had other claims on her attention. He looked back briefly into the Chinese salon where the Contessa was laughing at something the Barone Bobo had just said.

He was about to cross the Piazza when he noticed two other people observing the Contessa and the Barone. The dark Frenchwoman Marie Quimper gave a little start when she saw Urbino looking at her and her companion. Hugh Moss seemed unruffled.

"Mr. Macintyre, what a pleasant surprise!" Quimper said. She had a familiar volume under her arm.

"Isn't that *Baedeker's Northern Italy*?" Urbino asked. "The 1913 edition?"

Quimper gripped the book more tightly and exchanged a glance with Moss.

"Yes," Moss said, "the 1913 edition. It cost an arm and a leg."

"Well, it's worth it," Urbino said. "How long are you in Venice for?"

"Another week. I absolutely love Venice!" Quimper said with a quaver in her voice.

"Is this your first trip here?"

"We—"

"Our first and probably our last, considering the prices!" Moss interrupted gruffly. Without saying good-bye, he took Quimper's arm and almost dragged her toward the Molo.

Urbino and the Barone Bobo were hardly settled on the terrace of the Gritti Palace when the Barone said: "You don't like me, do you?"

Before Urbino could even consider his answer, the Barone added: "But what can a man of your refinement say? You would either have to lie or tell the bald, embarrassing truth. You're not the kind of person to do either with an easy conscience. I'm seldom wrong about people, and I have a feeling that neither are you. This puts us both in a difficult position, doesn't it?"

The Barone sipped his whiskey and took a deep breath of the cool, crisp air.

"But why quibble, especially here? Just look at this!" He threw out his hand at the waters of the Grand Canal, the creamy domes of the Salute, the Palazzo Dario leaning slightly to one side, the long white Guggenheim museum. The lights from the windows and boat landings shimmered in the water.

"A night for love," the Barone went on. "Perhaps you don't know that unreciprocated love brought one of your compatriots to throw herself from a window of that palazzo there and kill herself." He indicated a rose-colored building on the other side of the Grand Canal next to the *traghetto* station. "She loved one of your most famous writers, Henry James. But he was afraid of physical love. You can see it in what he wrote about D'Annunzio."

Urbino, who had more than a few things to say on the topic, remained silent. He hadn't come here tonight to discuss Henry James.

"Such a sad thing to be afraid of any manifestation of *l'amore*," the Barone added with a sympathetic shake of his head for all such souls.

A gondola with a man and woman glided past the Gritti Palace and approached the nearby landing. The man drew his companion's attention to the Gritti deck. The couple was Hugh Moss and his *belle-laide*, Marie Quimper. Urbino waved. Quimper waved back with a smile and Moss nodded sternly. If this had been any city other than Venice, with its web of waterways and serpentine *calles* providing innumerable and unexpected points of contact, Urbino might have found three encounters with this same couple unusual in one day. But he was accustomed to seeing the same faces many times in the space of only a few hours at scattered parts of town and on passing watercraft.

The Barone Bobo looked down at the couple as they got out of the gondola. He smiled.

"Two young lovers, you see. So wise to come to Venice in the autumn—the best season for her, don't you think? It suits her fading beauty."

"Autumn and Venice. A 'nuptial alliance,' D'Annunzio called it, didn't he?" Urbino said, hoping to turn the conversation to the threats. "I'm rereading *Fire*."

"To renew your pleasure or your disapproval? But that's unfair. I'm sure you're doing it for my sake. You want to be in the right mood for *Pomegranate*, yes? Unless you hope to catch me out in some misquoting!"

The Barone took a sip of whiskey and lit a Gauloise.

"I don't see why you keep suggesting that I have something against you, Barone."

"Bobo! 'Something against me'? An unusual way to put it. I said that I thought you don't like me. But I understand how you feel. Barbara has been giving me a lot of her attention. But don't forget we go back a long way, to when Alvise and my wife were alive. You shouldn't waste your fine energies wishing I weren't in Venice."

"Why did you want to see me tonight?" Urbino asked, with the air of someone trying his best to be patient.

"Why can't it just be to get to know you better, a good friend of Barbara's the way you are?"

"Because I think there's something more than that and something more than just rhapsodizing about the scene."

"Which is?"

"You tell me."

The Barone took a sip of his drink and looked directly into Urbino's eyes.

"It's Barbara," he said with a regretful air. "It's upsetting to have her so disturbed, and all because of something to do with me. I—I wanted to take this opportunity tonight, man to man as it were, to impress on you that it would be best not to trouble her with every little thing you might turn up or every idea you might have. In fact, if you learn anything, I'd appreciate it if you told me first."

"But you insist that the threats are of no consequence. If you really believe that, then there should be nothing to be worried about," Urbino observed with some satisfaction at pointing out the Barone's inconsistency.

"I'm *not* worried! Haven't you understood what I've been saying? It's Barbara I'm concerned about! You're being obstinate. Very well. Do as you wish, but if it takes any toll on Barbara, it will be your fault."

"My fault? Perhaps we can make some good use of our meeting here tonight if you're completely honest and tell me why you want to minimize the threats."

"Barbara—"

"Don't bring her into it! I'll begin to think you're using her as an excuse. It makes no sense not to be more concerned about yourself given the circumstances. I think you're *very* concerned. You know—or suspect—what or who is behind the threats, don't you?"

"I certainly do not! They're a prank, and that's the extent of them!"

"At Florian's today you seemed uneasy when I mentioned the man the guard saw lingering at the Doges' Palace," Urbino persisted.

"If I was acting 'uneasy,' it could only have been for Barbara's sake. She's more vulnerable than you believe. She might show you only her strong side—perhaps in response to something in you."

Urbino, who had no doubts about either the Contessa's vulnerability or her strength, returned to the point the Barone seemed intent on deflecting him from.

"You said that you had no idea who the man might be. He was about your age, tall, well dressed, and wore a brown fedora. Barbara said that *you* have a brown fedora."

"And so must hundreds—maybe thousands!—of men in this city. So you think I've been threatening myself! Barbara will thank you for *that*—if either of us is so stupid as to mention it to her." The Barone stood up abruptly. "I have an early rehearsal. I hope we understand each other. I'd appreciate it if you ended your inquiries. All this nosing around is just what the prankster probably wants. The drinks are on my account. Good evening."

The Barone strode into the hotel.

Urbino finished his drink as he looked out at the Grand Canal and thought about the Barone's desire for him to stop looking into the threats. Urbino had promised him nothing, but he would put things on hold until after the Barone's performance tomorrow evening. Of one thing he was absolutely certain, though. The Barone was afraid of something coming to light. Whether it was because he himself had made the threats or because something incriminating was behind them Urbino was determined to discover.

The next morning the Barone, without his brown fedora, went to the Doges' Palace. The young guard was sitting in the canvas chair next to the entrance of the Sala della Bussola. He immediately recognized the Barone.

The Barone spoke quietly with the guard for a few moments, then, with a glance around to confirm that no one could see them, the Barone took out a money clip and counted out several lira notes of a high denomination. The guard took them smoothly, slipped them into his pocket, and got up to make a circuit.

The Barone felt satisfied at a difficult transaction pulled off smoothly. He was about to retrace his steps to the entrance when he saw the Contessa's secretary, Harriet Kolb, coming down from the armory.

"Harriet! What a pleasant surprise. I never would have suspected that you had an interest in lances and crossbows!"

"Oh, I—I wasn't looking at those things," Harriet said. "I'm afraid I got lost. I—"

"Could you have been looking for the *bocca di leone?* It's right here."

"The *bocca di leone?*" Harriet looked confused. "I was looking for the Veroneses in the Sala del Collegio."

"You *are* lost, my dear! However do you find your way in the labyrinth of Venice? But you must have gone through the Sala del Collegio on your way in."

He gave her directions to the room she said she was seeking and then said: "Harriet, I'd appreciate it if you didn't say anything to the Contessa about seeing me here." He put a hand on her wrist. "You know how concerned she is about the threats. One of them was left in the *bocca* here, as you know. I wouldn't want her to think I was worried." He gave a dry little laugh that was more like a cough. "She'd be on pins and needles all during my performances, thinking I was abstracted. We wouldn't want her disturbed, would we?"

"Of course not, Barone," Kolb said, keeping her eyes averted.

"And please, my dear. Don't stand on ceremony. Just call me Bobo."

He gave her wrist a slight pressure and released her with a smile. Harriet hurried away, passing through the Sala della Bussola without even a glance at either the *bocca di leone* or the guard.

Out in Piazza San Marco the Barone decided against a coffee at Florian's. It would make him late for his rehearsal. Livia, his director, was one of the people he least wanted to provoke, having had ample evidence of the power of her wrath. He walked briskly through the Piazza toward the Teatro del Ridotto. From a window table at Caffè Quadri someone watched his progress with a cold satisfied smile.

Urbino, sitting next to the Contessa, was actually enjoying Bobo's performance. The Contessa need have no fear that he would "dry up." Quite the contrary. He was very impressively flowing along. In fact, his performance was so operatic that a more appropriate venue might have been the Teatro La Fenice instead of the intimate Teatro del Ridotto. Bobo's *Pomegranate*, like D'Annunzio himself, as Oriana's account at Harry's Bar had made clear, was pure Verdi.

What Urbino wasn't enjoying, however, was the rapt look on the Contessa's face and the smile she occasionally turned in his direction, as if to say, Isn't he marvelous! What more could we ask for?

They could ask for very little more, Urbino had to admit. Somehow Bobo managed, with the aid of only minimal makeup, to transform himself into the gnomelike D'Annunzio as he moved from one episode of the writer's melodramatic life to another. What had Oriana said? We want to be deceived? Well, Bobo was doing an excellent job of it.

It was during the scenes describing Venice and the aging beauty of La Foscarina—the character based on the actress Eleonora Duse—that the Contessa seemed most entranced. She stared at the stage as if she could see the two lovers gliding in a gondola down the Grand Canal in the full glory of autumn.

"The Palace of the Cornaro and the Palace of the Pesaro passed them, like two opaque giants blackened by time as by the smoke of a conflagration," said Bobo in his sonorous stage voice, which was a perfect vehicle for D'Annunzio's words. *"The Ca' d'Oro passed them like a divine play of stone and air; then the Rialto showed its ample back already noisy with popular life, laden with its encumbered shops, filled with the odor of fish and vegetables, like an enormous cornucopia pouring on the shore all round it an abundance of the fruits of the earth and sea with which to feed the dominant city.*

"Do not all fragile souls come here as to a place of refuge, those who hide some secret wound, those who have accomplished some final renunciation, those whom a morbid love has emasculated, and those who only seek silence the better to hear themselves perish? Perhaps Venice is in their eyes a clement city of death, embraced by a sleep-giving pool.

"Does it not strike you that we seem to be following the princely

retinue of dead Summer? There she lies in her funeral boat, all dressed in gold like the wife of a Doge. And the procession is taking her to the Island of Murano, where some masterly Lord of Fire will make her a crystal coffin. And the walls of the coffin shall be of opal, so that once submerged in the Laguna, she may at least see the languid play of the seaweed through her transparent eyelids, and while awaiting the hour of resurrection give herself the illusion of having still about her person the constant undulation of her voluptuous hair."

Then more intimately: "*Of all your loving person I love the delicate lines that go from your eyes to your temples, and the little dark veins that make violets of your eyelids, and the undulation of your cheek, and your weary chin, and all that in you seems touched by the disease of Autumn and all that is shadow on your passionate face.*"

The Contessa gave a silent but nonetheless perceptible sigh and whispered to Urbino, her face slightly flushed: "Ah! Bobo *is* D'Annunzio."

And with this praise—rather dubious, considering D'Annunzio's scandalous reputation—the Contessa returned her attention to the Barone Bobo.

The *salone da ballo* at the Ca' da Capo-Zendrini had been transformed by draperies of gold and purple—the Barone Bobo's favorite colors—by standing candelabra and hanging torches in bronze baskets that caught the melting wax, and by what the Contessa called the "Pomegranate Centerpiece" on the buffet table.

This was the head of a woman, fashioned from autumn vegetables and fruits in the manner of Archimboldo. It represented

Persephone, banished forever to the underworld after eating a few seeds of the pomegranate. This fruit—which D'Annunzio's hero in *Fire* assumed as his mysterious emblem—predominated in the centerpiece and on the buffet table: firm orbs of them, sliced halves and wedges that exposed their crimson flesh, goblets of Murano crystal overflowing with their fatal seeds and dripping their juice that stained the cloth.

Waiters in black tuxedos passed drinks and canapés while a chamber orchestra, on a platform beneath the sixteenth-century tapestry of Susanna and the Elders, played Vivaldi and Debussy. The crisp scent of the autumn night came through the open doors of the loggia overlooking the Grand Canal and mingled with the aromas of myrrh, musk, and amber burning in bronze chafing dishes.

Urbino excused himself from a group the Barone was charming with his gallant conversation and slipped out to the loggia. He spent several restorative minutes looking out at the scene. The liquid boulevard of the Grand Canal reflected the sweep of illuminated palazzi on each bank down to the sharp bend of the Grand Canal, where, over the Rialto Bridge, a bright full moon seemed placed for maximum effect. A passing vaporetto sent ripples lapping against the palazzo's garden wall and the blue-and-white-striped mooring poles of the water steps. The sound of laughter and a snatch of song floated up from a passing gondola.

He was about to return to the *salone* when Marco Zeoli and Harriet Kolb came out. The assistant medical director, wearing a nondescript dark suit, looked as dour and unhealthy as usual, but the plain Harriet was dressed with care and attention in a long dust-colored dress in Indian cotton. This evening, glowing with something more than just the careful application of makeup, her receding chin and slightly protruding teeth were less evident. Could the object of her affections be not the Barone, but Zeoli? It seemed a more appropriate match.

They spent a few moments chatting about the Barone's performance, then Zeoli said that it was unfortunate that Urbino had had to cut short his therapy.

"If he stopped eating foods with nightshade as I told him last week he might not need any therapy at all," Harriet said. "But I don't mean anything against the spa, Marco. After all, I'll be coming there for the week between Christmas and New Year's. That is, if I can save up enough money by then."

Harriet had an excellent salary but she always seemed strapped for money. The Contessa said she threw away a lot on palm readers, chiropractors, and long-distance calls to a card-reader cum nutritionist in London. She was now talking about her chiropractor in Dorsoduro.

"And he kept putting this ugly indentation in my neck! You can still see it. Look, Marco."

She bent her head.

"I don't see anything, Harriet."

"Well, I *feel* it!" She rubbed her neck with a little frown. "And I don't know why, but after every session my eyeballs were as dry as marbles. I promised Barbara I'd stay through the winter but I'm afraid the dampness is going to coax my lumbago right out in the open. And the bridges! Until you come here you don't know that they're really *steps*. It jars your whole system, day after day, day after day."

Urbino knew that the expression on his face couldn't be as patient as the one on Zeoli's. Zeoli had almost fifteen years' experience with people like Harriet.

"—and after taking the bicarbonate the *other* doctor prescribed, my stomach swelled up like someone was blowing up a balloon. The flesh in the area was tender and my ribs felt on fire. But then this new doctor rolled me like a piece of dough and something popped. I started to feel better right away. Two years before—"

Urbino was trying to find some way of escape when Oriana sailed out to the loggia with John Flint, Hugh Moss, and Marie Quimper in tow.

"So this is where you've been hiding," Oriana said, looking strident in her Versace outfit. "Barbara is cross with you. You haven't met Bobo's brother-in-law or Livia." Livia Festa was Bobo's director. "Be careful of Livia, though. She's got her fingers out for money to make a film of *Pomegranate*."

"Ridiculous!" Moss said. His untidy hair seemed to crackle with emotion and his thin lips were twisted into a scar. "A movie! The Barone would be revealed for just what he is. A caricature!"

There were a few moments of silence, broken first by Oriana's operatic laugh. Then Quimper gave a little cry that seemed to be fright but soon revealed itself to be her version of enthusiasm: "Oh, my! The purple sky and the golden lights of the palaces! Just like the Contessa's color scheme. You should try to paint it, Hugh. Oh, it's really a dream! How could anyone help being in love here?"

Moss didn't seem to hear her. His eyes were searching the crowded ballroom until they lighted on the Barone, now in close conversation with the manager of the Teatro del Ridotto. They seemed to be exchanging sharp words. Moss's stare was hard.

Agreement with Quimper came from a somewhat unlikely quarter.

"Oh yes," Harriet said, "so many people say that Venice and death go together, but it's really Venice and love."

"Maybe it's Venice, love, *and* death," Flint drawled. "I just read that Wagner wrote the 'Liebestod' of *Tristan und Isolde* in his palazzo on the Grand Canal. Love-death, death-in-love, love's-death, and all that."

Harriet looked wounded. Flint, with a self-conscious shrug that showed off the lines of his Comme-des-Garçons suit to finer advantage, said: "Speaking of palazzos, I had my nose pressed up against the gate of yours this afternoon, Urbino."

"And speaking of *noses*," Oriana said, "your sweet little one is dripping." She took out a handkerchief and handed it to him. "Just like the boy you are! If you don't get rid of that cold soon, we're going straight to Marco's spa for a month."

Flint dabbed at his nose with Oriana's handkerchief, which had sent an expensive scent drifting through the air.

"Quite a jewel, your palazzo," Flint went on. "Too bad it isn't on the Grand Canal. Veneto-Byzantine, isn't it?"

"But don't you remember, John?" Oriana said. "I told you—and Hugh and Marie—all about it. It was built by some crackpot—no relation to Urbino!—back in the seventeenth century, long after the days of the Byzantine."

"But that lacy marble fretwork looks just like the Doges' Palace," Flint persisted, "and the big window on the second story must once have had polylobate piercings. And what about . . ."

Flint quickly demonstrated, in considerable detail and with a self-important air, that he knew exactly what he was talking about.

"I was wondering," he said, "if you have a mysterious room like the one here."

"I'm afraid not."

"A mysterious room?" Marie Quimper said.

"Yes, dear," Oriana said. "The Caravaggio Room."

"Tell us about it, Monsieur Macintyre!"

"The room is named after a Caravaggio that has hung in it since the twenties," he began. He then described how people sleeping in the room had met mysterious or unusual deaths, all of them members of the Da Capo-Zendrini family by birth or marriage. The last death—this one of a beautiful young woman—took place in the late thirties during the course of a house party. The Contessa refused to use the room.

"It's only a few doors away from mine," Kolb said with a quaver in her voice. "I feel a strange aura coming from it sometimes when I pass. And my psychic told me to beware of locked doors!"

"Don't be absurd, Harriet!" scoffed Oriana, who found everyone's superstitions but her own ludicrous. "It's a room like any other and one of these days Barbara will see how silly she's being. We have to convince her, Urbino."

"If anyone could convince the Contessa," Quimper said, "it would be someone like yourself, Monsieur Macintyre. You're the kind of person one instinctively trusts. I felt it as soon as I saw your photograph on the jacket of the Proust book. You looked—"

"Don't make a fool of yourself, Marie!" Moss broke in, grabbing her elbow more roughly than was necessary.

"Beware the monster jealousy, Hugh," Oriana chided. "Remember, this is the city of Othello. I thought you'd bite off poor Marie's head when she asked John for a picture from his modeling days. It will drive sweet little Marie away—or much worse! You can give us a sad example, Marco. What about that poor woman slaughtered in one of your treatment rooms?"

It would be difficult to say who was more upset by her words—Moss, who looked as if he wanted to slap her, or Zeoli, whose sallow face had paled. The assistant medical director mumbled something about the impeccable reputation of his spa and excused himself.

10

When Urbino finally met Orlando Gava and Livia Festa half an hour later, Urbino recognized Gava as the "Roman senator" from the Abano pool. Gava gave no indication that he remembered Urbino, however. With his moon-shaped, unhealthily flushed face, pendulous lower lip, and drooping eyes, he was as homely as the Barone was handsome. He wore a black crepe armband. Sadness seemed to emanate from him in dark, powerful waves.

In contrast to Gava, Livia Festa radiated health and good spirits. She had a plumpness suggestive of an odalisque pampered in a sultan's harem. Dyed-red hair sprang from beneath a black lacy snood, and a dark green silk robe, with a cabalistic design across the top, bestowed the look of a priestess. A cape had been thrown over an armchair to accommodate a small white dog.

"I leave the renegade to you both," the Contessa said, stunning in a gold silk bias-cut Vionnet, "but I warn you, Livia dear: Don't try to squeeze any money out of the poor boy. He lives far beyond his means. I have to go off to convince those men over there that having their boats diverted by my bridge of boats isn't the same as sending them around the Cape of Good Hope!"

When the Contessa had left, Festa said in a smoke-hoarse voice: "This is my little baby. His name is Peppino."

She took a treat for Peppino from her purse. He gave it a few unenthusiastic nibbles.

"You write biographies," said Gava dolefully, as if this must be the saddest endeavor imaginable. "Barbara says you're good at it—and at solving crimes, too. You're looking into the threats against Bobo."

"Bobo told us the other night at dinner," Festa quickly explained. "He joked about them but I'm sure he's upset."

"Oh, he's upset," Gava said. "I knew it as soon as he said he wasn't. Actors! You always have to assume they mean the opposite of what they say."

"Spoken just like a man of business! Orlando has some factories in Torino that make him a bundle of money!" Festa explained for Urbino's benefit. "I think I'm a better judge of actors, Orlando dear. They're more like children than anything else."

Suddenly, over the music and the other voices, came Bobo's magisterial voice: "*Dama Venezia* is a beautiful corpse, giving off the flush of the grave. Camille of the waves, the consumptive heroine of the sea, the painted lady of—"

They looked in Bobo's direction. He was the center of a group of admiring women.

"Well, he acted the spoiled child often enough with my poor sister, may God rest her soul! She never complained, not even at the very end, as you remember."

Gava touched his armband and tears welled in his eyes. Festa considered him with an inscrutable look that might have been irritation or uneasiness, then started to chatter about D'Annunzio and the Barone's miraculous reincarnation of him.

"D'Annunzio!" Gava almost spat it out. "Rosa couldn't bear to hear his name mentioned! An immoral man!"

Gava's raised voice drew a long stare from Bobo.

"D'Annunzio was mentioned in the threats," Urbino said when Bobo returned his attention to the women with evident reluctance. "Do you have any idea who might be responsible for them?"

"Not me, if that's what you're thinking," Gava said.

"Orlando!" Festa remonstrated. "That wasn't what he was thinking at all. If he suspects anyone it's me!"

"You? But you like D'Annunzio, too, and—and you like Bobo. You were going to marry him!"

"What I meant," Festa said, "is that it's great publicity—or *would* be if it got into the papers."

Festa described publicity stunts she was familiar with from her years at Cinecittà. Urbino let his eye wander around the room. The orchestra was now playing popular tunes and guests swept across the floor. Flint executed perfect steps with Oriana only a few feet away from Filippo, her husband, who was less smoothly but no less enthusiastically dancing with an American divorcée. Groups formed and dispersed according to the laws and whims that regulate such gatherings. The people lounging on sofas and chairs set against the walls seemed reluctant, either from comfort or inertia, to get up, and eyed those who were dancing or standing with the air of bored royalty.

Festa was finishing her reminiscences when the Contessa came up and, with a barely audible apology, led Urbino away.

"More trouble," she said when they were out of earshot of anyone. "Another threat against Bobo. The manager from the Teatro del Ridotto just told me. Bobo wanted it kept a secret. The box office attendant found one of those sheets in the lobby before the performance. You must try harder to get to the bottom of this."

"I don't know what Bobo has told you, but he made it very clear to me that he doesn't want me snooping around."

"He doesn't know what he's saying! He needs you. We both do. See into his heart. There you'll find his *real* feelings about this whole thing! Bobo—"

"Is something the matter, Barbara?"

It was Harriet, who had come upon them unnoticed. A slick film of moisture coated her forehead.

"Nothing at all, my dear. Excuse me."

The Contessa hurried off to join the Barone, who was now talking to the theater manager again. A short distance away Festa was making flamboyant gestures at a Milanese industrialist while Gava stared straight ahead gloomily as if he were at his beloved sister's funeral. Even from this distance the melancholy surrounding the Barone's brother-in-law was a thick, dark curtain.

Harriet pulled a small handkerchief from her sleeve and gently wiped her forehead.

"How close it is in here! All this incense is cutting off my oxygen and the burning wax is making my eyes burn. I'll have to go up to my room and put in some eyedrops."

Before she left, Urbino asked her for one of Bobo's publicity photographs.

A few minutes later, when Bobo, with less composure than usual, began to recite D'Annunzio's prayer-prologue for Debussy's *Martyrdom of St. Sebastian* to a musical accompaniment, Urbino went down to the garden.

He walked through a courtyard of Venetian brick and past statues of chained Turks in Istrian stone up to the higher level. A pebbled path lined with clipped boxwood, laurel hedges, and stone mythological figures took him toward a pergola. The pergola, sheltering a Roman bath and covered with Virginia creeper and English ivy, was the Contessa's and Urbino's favorite place in the garden.

Raised, angry voices coming from the pergola stopped him short. They were those of a man and a woman, but he couldn't make out who they were. Ironically, he might have been better able to hear if he had been farther away from the pergola. The garden had unusual acoustics, which it shared with Venice itself where sound traveled erratically and mysteriously.

Afraid that whoever it was might abruptly leave the shelter of the pergola to find him eavesdropping, he returned along the pebbled path to the lower level and sat in a wicker chair. After five minutes Quimper and Moss appeared. Quimper was the first to see Urbino.

"Monsieur Macintyre! I wish we knew you were here! You could have given us a tour." She touched one of the stone Turks. "Gardens come as such a pleasant surprise in Venice. Do you have one? If it's anything like this one, you're very fortunate. I have only a little patch of ground off my kitchen in London but back in Paris I had a lovely garden."

She seemed about to continue, if only because she didn't know how to stop, when Moss, his face still in the shadows, reminded her that they had to be on their way.

When Urbino came through the doors of the *salone*, a low buzz of concerned voices had replaced the music, and the musicians and guests were staring at the far end of the room. There, a knot of people had formed. Among them was the Contessa, looking very distressed. Urbino hurried over. Gava lay prostrate on the floor near a broken water goblet, his eyes closed and his face colorless. An elderly physician from Padua, one of the Contessa's guests, was kneeling by Gava's side. Peppino looked down at the scene from a chair covered with his mistress's reversed cape.

"I—I just gave him a drink of water and he collapsed," Festa said.

"He has asthma and emphysema, just like his sister had," Bobo said.

The physician loosened Gava's tie and unbuttoned the top of his shirt. He waved away a glass of water brought by Flint.

"Oh, I hope he didn't eat any of the shrimp or drink red wine, Signora Festa!" said Harriet, almost as white as Gava. "People with his condition are usually severely allergic to them, aren't they, Doctor? Iodine and sulfites."

Festa glared at her.

"It *is* close in here," Bobo said. "Perhaps the incense choked him up. It was doing the same to you, Harriet."

"Oh, I hope it wasn't my incense!" the Contessa lamented. "Harriet, call an ambulance."

Before rushing off, Harriet thrust a large envelope into Urbino's hand.

Gava regained consciousness and tried to raise his head. He looked confusedly at the faces peering down at him. He focused on Bobo.

"Rosa, my dear sister," he said before passing out again. "I'm coming."

The next morning, after the Contessa called to tell him that Gava was doing fairly well and was recuperating in his room at the Flora, Urbino went to the Teatro del Ridotto to inquire about the threat left in the foyer.

"It had to be before seven," the theater manager said. "The box office attendant noticed it when he returned from a break. I called the police immediately. We've added an extra guard for the rest of the Barone's run."

Urbino next went to the Doges' Palace with the Barone's publicity photograph. The guard took one quick look at it and shook his head.

"Nothing like the man."

He handed the photograph back.

"Are you sure? This is about ten years old but the man looks very much the same."

"He's not the one who was here. Excuse me. I have to make my circuit."

Urbino slipped the photograph back in the envelope. The guard's response puzzled him. He had been too abrupt in dismissing the photograph and no longer seemed to want to talk about the incident.

Urbino wouldn't have had any doubts if the guard had identified the Barone. Was this because he was convinced that Bobo had been at the Doges' Palace or because he was so biased against him that he *wanted* him to have been?

He could see two rocks looming dangerously in the waters of his inquiries. One was his friendship with the Contessa, for whom he would do almost anything. The other was his dislike of the Barone. But why, precisely? Because the Contessa admired him and enjoyed spending time with him, might even be falling in love with him? Because Urbino's comfortable relationship with her was endangered?

Or did he sense something essentially false about the man? Actors often possessed an affected manner that had nothing to do with insincerity but was sometimes merely the fruit of discipline. Was this what he was responding to in Bobo?

He must be careful. Yet not so careful that he went too far in the opposite direction and wrote off suspicion as mere unfounded prejudice. No, it wasn't going to be easy.

That afternoon Urbino hurried over a bridge near Piazza San Marco, where gondoliers in their straw hats and striped shirts were calling out to tourists. The autumn weather was today more gray than golden. A few drops of warm rain fell as he ducked into the Libreria Sangiorgio.

Bobo was enthroned behind a table with copies of *Pomegranate* and *I See the Sun*. A group of people, neither vulgarly large nor embarrassingly small, waited to have him sign their books. Among them were a tense-looking Marie Quimper and her companion, Hugh Moss.

"Urbino dear!" the Contessa called. Radiant in copper-hued silk that subtly complemented Bobo's tweeds, she stood beside him, one hand on his shoulder, the other holding an extra Mont Blanc, just as she did at Urbino's own signings here. Urbino bought a copy of the two books and got at the end of the line behind Oriana and Flint. Flint seemed jumpy and his eyes were dilated.

"For my folks back home," he said, indicating the books in his arms. "Though they certainly don't know Italian and never even heard of this D'Annunzio guy."

"That describes half the people here, I'm sure," Oriana said. The two burst into laughter. Oriana's laugh was her usual operatic one, but Flint's sounded askew, as if he wasn't in control of it. Livia Festa frowned. She kept shooting glances at the Barone and the Contessa—glances which, if they had been given by one of her own actors, she would most likely have asked to be brought down a few notches, even for the stage.

When their fit of laughter was over, Flint handed Urbino the books in his arms. He dashed through the rain and into the Bauer-Grünwald Hotel on the other side of the bridge.

When he returned ten minutes later, an interval Oriana filled with anecdotes about the Philistinism of Filippo's family, he said: "Well, Urbino, when are you going to invite me into your inner sanctum?"

He gave his laugh again, which was slightly out of control, his eyes even more dilated now. Urbino saw no way out but to ask him to stop by after the signing. When Oriana, pleased at the apparent rapport between the two men, resumed her anecdotes, Urbino was free to consider the others in the room.

The person he was most surprised to see was Marco Zeoli, who had a full schedule at the thermal spa. Perhaps he had come to be with Harriet, who, however, was standing by herself. If she was indeed in love, today she seemed to be suffering the predictable pains of that state. Like one for whom true love was not running smoothly, she seemed to be finding the enamored states of others unbearable. She scrutinized the Contessa and the Barone with particular discomfort. The one person she didn't look at was Zeoli, a sign that he was the probable source of her affliction.

Urbino shared Harriet's feelings of exclusion as he approached the table. It wasn't that he wanted to deny the Contessa the gratifications of the heart. He couldn't quite bring himself to call them, even less to think of them, as the gratifications of the flesh. But the Barone wasn't a worthy object of her affections. Instead he seemed the kind of man to take full advantage of them.

Bobo gave Urbino a broad smile when his turn came, and signed the books with a flourish.

"I hope you're coming to closing night tomorrow. We'd miss you, wouldn't we, Barbarina?" He smiled up at the Contessa. "I always have one special person in the audience to act for. Of course, it will be Barbara, but if you're there, too, it will be an added inspiration."

"Of course he'll come! And afterward we'll have a nightcap at the Ca' da Capo," the Contessa said before going off to join Oriana and Flint, who were paging through a book on Venetian jewelry.

Festa, who was standing close enough to the table to have heard this interchange, picked up the Baron Corvo's *Desire and Pursuit of the Whole*, opened it at random, and started to read with furious attention. After assuring Bobo that he would try to make the closing performance, Urbino joined Festa.

"Impossible book!" she said with more animosity for the eccentric novel of Venice than seemed warranted. "My English isn't up to it—or my patience!"

She slammed the book down.

"A strange book, I admit," Urbino said, wondering if it was in his power to calm the woman down before she turned over the whole display, "but I've grown to like it. He's buried over on San Michele. His real name was Frederick Rolfe. He wasn't a real baron, you know."

Involuntarily they looked at Bobo. Moss had taken advantage of Bobo's momentary solitary state to have a few private words with him. Quimper stood alone against a bookshelf, watching Bobo and Moss with acute anxiety.

"Bobo's a *real* barone, though," Festa said. "For what that's worth. Excuse me. I must go."

One of the owners of the bookshop came over to Urbino with copies of his books and asked him to inscribe them. They talked about Ruskin as Urbino guardedly watched Moss and the Barone. Moss was saying something to him. The Barone stiffened, looked intensely into Moss's face, and said something in his turn. Moss answered back. Then they both looked at the Contessa. The Barone stood up abruptly as Moss walked toward her. Before he could reach her, however, Quimper grabbed his sleeve in passing and they retired against one of the bookshelves.

Suddenly Oriana gave a little cry. She and Flint were looking at a sheet of paper in her hand. The Contessa snatched it away and stuck it into the book on jewelry and clapped the book shut. She looked over at Urbino, who excused himself and joined her.

"He's struck again!" Urbino would almost have laughed at the Contessa's exclamation except for the pained look on her face.

"Another threat! The same as the others. Oriana found it on the bookshelf. Oh, Urbino! I thought you were going to put a stop to all this!"

An hour later Urbino and Flint were in the library of the Palazzo Uccello. On the way from the bookshop, they had talked about the latest threat, coming to no conclusions. But now Flint's interest was obviously only for the little palazzo.

He appreciatively took in the rows of books, the paintings, the refectory table, and the dark wood confessional where Urbino's cat Serena was napping. Then he noticed the collection of six-teenth-century Venetian books. He examined them closely.

"I know someone who would give you a small fortune for these. If you're ever interested in selling any of them, let me know," Flint said slowly, prolonging every single vowel.

Flint seemed to be the kind of Southerner who thought he could charm the world if he only drawled. It had much the oppo-site effect on Urbino, who was, however, perhaps unfairly preju-diced against the handsome man on this point, as on others. Urbino, with probably just as much deliberation as Flint, had made a contrary effort to banish his own New Orleans accent.

"I wouldn't sell the least of them. They're a gift," Urbino said.

"From Barbara, of course. Yes, women are sensitive when it comes to selling their gifts, but a gift no longer belongs to the giver once it's out of her hands."

Urbino held his tongue as he led Flint into the parlor. At first it was the baroque stucco ceiling that caught Flint's attention. Then he scrutinized the Bronzino portrait of a pearl-and-brocaded Florentine lady over the sofa.

"A generous woman, isn't she?" Flint said, at first confusing

Urbino, who found the Bronzino woman more angular than ample. "Oriana has a big heart, too, but not as big a pocketbook. If I didn't know that you inherited this place, I would have thought that Barbara had turned it over to you because she didn't know what else to do with it."

"Let me make something clear. Barbara and I are only friends."

"One can always hope for more—but perhaps not now with the Barone in the picture."

Flint took out a silk handkerchief and wiped his nose, which had started to drip during the past few minutes. A network of broken capillaries marred its perfection.

"This place is small, though. When people hear you live in a palazzo, they must expect something like Barbara's place."

"It's big enough for me." Urbino hoped they could leave the Contessa out of the conversation. "I've turned the top floor over to my housekeeper and her husband. I live on only this floor."

"What about the ground floor? Damp and flooded?"

"Not at all. I'm using it for an art restoration workshop. I'm just an amateur, though. I restored the portrait of the Cremonese lady you saw in the library."

"Another gift from Barbara, I'm sure. By the way, Oriana wasn't clear about how you inherited the building."

"From my mother's side of the family," Urbino said, trying to keep his patience. "She never saw it, unfortunately. She was born in New Orleans, always intended to go to Italy, but never did. It's been a bit of a struggle to keep it up, with the restoration and the repairs and everything else. I do what I can but I have to let a lot of things go. If you look closely you'll see what I mean. The chandelier has a lot of pieces missing, and those portraits on the other wall need to be cleaned."

"You're breaking my heart! Less than perfect Murano chandeliers and dirty portraits!"

"They're all by minor Venetian painters."

"Yes, but the frames alone are works of art. They could bring in a pretty penny. But I've already taken up enough of your time,

Urbino. Don't forget now. If you ever change your mind about those books, I could put enough money in your hands so that you could make more than a few repairs around here! I feel so sorry for you having to live amid such squalor!"

On the closing night of *Pomegranate* some of the fog invading the city seemed to have crept into Bobo's performance, which was vague and distracted.

"I have some things to see to, Barbara," Bobo said afterward. "I'll join you and Urbino in an hour."

During the trip up the Grand Canal, where the fog was swirling in thick patches, the Contessa made only perfunctory remarks and eventually the two friends fell silent. But when the door of the *salotto blu* was closed behind them, the Contessa said in a flat, dead voice: "Something's wrong. I saw it in Bobo's eyes. He was planning to come right back. Maybe it's another threat! You must have noticed that his performance was off."

She kept glancing at the mantel clock. Usually she nursed her wine but this evening she drank it quickly and refilled her glass. She moved restlessly about the room, but expended little of her energy in conversation. Urbino paged through magazines, content just to be her silent, understanding companion, but as the time dragged he began to feel as if he were keeping vigil with her.

Bobo didn't show up after an hour, or an hour and a half. There was no word, no call. The Contessa's nervousness eventually began to affect Urbino. It was a quarter to midnight when Lucia said that the Contessa was wanted on the phone. The Contessa hurriedly left the room, having banished telephones from her *salotto*.

"How very strange," she said when she returned. "That young artist,

Hugh Moss, of all people! He insists on stopping by at this ungodly hour! He sounded drunk. Whatever does he want to see *me* for?"

"At Bobo's signing yesterday he was going to come over to you but his girlfriend restrained him. And right before that when Moss was talking to him, Bobo seemed frightened and Moss looked as if he—"

He trailed off. How could he describe Moss during those moments with Bobo?

"Looked as if he what?" the Contessa said impatiently.

"As if he enjoyed seeing Bobo uncomfortable, as if that was why he was talking with him and saying whatever it was he was saying. And then there was the way they both looked at you, as if you were very much a part of Moss's enjoyment and—and Bobo's fear and discomfort."

"You've been reading too much Henry James! Such volumes in a conversation you didn't hear a word of! Quimper said something the other night about Moss wanting to paint my portrait and maybe the view from the loggia. That's the extent of it, I'm sure."

For the next forty-five minutes the Contessa retired into a silent sulk from which she withdrew only when footsteps sounded in the hall.

"Bobo!" she said and jumped up.

But it wasn't Bobo. It was Harriet, with a knit cap pulled down on her forehead and looking exhausted. She seemed to be out of breath.

"Harriet! Are you coming in or going out?"

"Coming in. I—I was at Marco's. I got lost in the fog. Good night."

The Contessa returned to her chair and lapsed back into her own gloomy thoughts. Urbino wondered if they were going to sit like this all night.

But once again, ten minutes later, footsteps sounded in the hall. This time it was Bobo. He stood at the door of the *salotto* and looked in as if searching for someone or something and fearful of what he would find. The Contessa went up to his side, her face at first smiling with relief, then drawing into a horrified expression.

"Bobo! You're bleeding!"

Indeed, blood stained one end of his scarf. He looked down at it as if it had absolutely nothing to do with him.

On the other side of the Grand Canal a tourist lost her way as she hurried back to her hotel. Her head was filled with terrifying images.

Were his lips sliced off as well as his nose and ears?

She couldn't remember. She had tried not to pay attention, but now she knew, as she stumbled through the fog and darkness, that it had done little good.

Skinned alive, of that she was sure, but had that nasty little man in the church actually said something about the skin being stuffed with earth—or was it straw?—and being displayed through the streets on a cow?

"And it's right in there," he said, pointing to the urn beneath the bust of the ill-fated general.

"What is?"

"The skin! We stole it from the damn Turks!"

She had thrust some lire into his hands and rushed from the church. Now the memory of the encounter and the fear that the man might be following her had made her lose her way in the maze of alleys.

She stopped. Should she continue straight on or turn left or right? She had crossed over the Rialto Bridge a few minutes ago, surprised to find how deserted the area was. In the daytime it was bustling with shops and kiosks selling souvenirs and vegetables.

She heard footsteps behind her, but rather than being relieved, she was more frightened than before. Surely it must be the man from the church! She turned impulsively to her right and hurried over the slippery stones. The fog and the darkness were even thicker here. She stopped after a few moments and listened. Just as she feared, the footsteps made the same turn.

She ran. Out of breath, the blood pounding in her ears, she found herself in an enclosed area, with what looked like cages around her. For a few moments she thought she had wandered into a zoo, but the city didn't have a zoo, did it? And she didn't hear any animals, thank God. The pursuing footsteps were now silent. What she did hear was the lapping of water and a boat chugging by, then a woman's distant laughter. Reassured, she gave a little laugh herself at her own foolishness.

She would walk toward the woman's laughter. There she would find light and life. She turned too quickly and lost her footing on something slippery. She fell to her knees and her purse flew from her. On her hands and knees she groped along the paving stones for it. She touched leather but it wasn't her purse, but something smaller, with harder edges. She withdrew her hand quickly. What was it? Fearfully, tentatively, she reached out again. This time she didn't touch leather but the fingers of a hand. She screamed and leaped up.

She could now see a dark figure lying on the stones. It didn't move. She ran only a short distance before she tripped and fell again.

A few inches from her face was another face—or what was left of it. It was now a mass of blood and tissue. Her hands slipped on something wet. She brought one hand up to her face. A small object was sticking to her palm. A pebble, she thought. She picked it from her palm and was about to throw it back on the pavement when she looked at it more closely.

Horrified, she realized what it was. A tooth.

PART TWO

The Pomegranate Tree

1

Next morning Urbino and the Contessa, not yet aware of the deaths on the Rialto that would affect their lives so deeply, were sitting in the Contessa's *salotto blu*. The Contessa was idling paging through D'Annunzio's *Fire*.

"Bobo's upstairs. We checked him out of the Gritti," she added, with a slight tilt to her chin. "The threat at the signing hit him hard, but he's being stoic."

"Did he say where he was last night?"

"He and Livia had a drink at Harry's, then he went for a walk. It's all that unused energy after a performance."

"And the nosebleed?"

"Part of his exuberance, I'm sure." Having delivered this questionable medical opinion, she took a sip of tea and picked up the D'Annunzio novel again. When she finished a passage and looked up to find Urbino's eyes on her, she said: "What a peculiar look! I'm not exactly reading *Lady Chatterley's Lover*! And I don't approve of everything D'Annunzio did—or wrote. But it's his passion that captures me. He was passionate about so many things—and passion is one of the most important qualities, don't you think? Passion and honesty—is there anything else?"

"No, Barbarina," came the Barone Bobo's voice from the door, less hearty than usual, "there isn't—unless it's love!"

"Bobo! I hope you found nooks and crannies for all your things."

"Oh, somehow I managed," he said with a forced laugh. His eyes were pocketed with fatigue. He walked over to the bar and poured himself an anisette. When he raised the glass to his lips, a few drops of the clear liquid spattered his white shirtfront.

"Orlando is coming along fine," the Contessa said. "I was talking with him earlier. I told him that we would all be remembering Rosa on the Day of All Souls. She died around then, didn't she? What day was it exactly?"

"The twenty-eighth or the twenty-ninth. I—I forget." Then with more conviction: "She died late at night, you see. Right before or after midnight."

He finished his anisette. Astonishment briefly touched the Contessa's face. She was a woman who knew not only the year and the day but the precise hour of the deaths of her loved ones. Her decision to revive the old Venetian tradition of the bridge of boats to the cemetery island on the Day of All Souls came as much from this deep reverence for the dead as from her love for all things Venetian. Her eyes flicked in Urbino's direction before she said: "Yes, it's sometimes difficult to remember painful memories, I find. The mind just shuts down." Then, with more energy and a rueful smile at Bobo: "But whatever the precise date, it means that our procession will have all that more meaning. We'll all be remembering Rosa. She always seemed like such a dear woman."

It was Bobo's opportunity to make up for his lapse of memory, but he said nothing.

Before anyone might break the uncomfortable silence, the door of the *salotto blu* burst open. It was Oriana and Flint.

"If you're calmly sitting here like that with a book in your lap, Barbara, then you can't possibly have heard the terrible news." Oriana settled herself with a great deal of histrionics in one of the Louis Quinze chairs. "Tell them, John dear. I'm emotionally exhausted. This has been one of the worst days of my life."

Flint cast an appraising glance over the furnishings and bibelots.

"Oriana isn't exaggerating. It *is* bad news. We just found out at the Flora."

"Orlando!" the Contessa said, standing up. "Oh, don't tell me the poor man is dead!"

"Orlando? Dead?"

Bobo's voice held a strange note. Flint was studying the Barone's reaction with peculiar interest. Before Oriana or Flint might further enlighten them, raised voices sounded from the hallway, followed by footsteps.

An olive-skinned man in his late forties, dressed in a dark gray suit and tie, appeared in the doorway next to Mauro, the majordomo. Behind them was a blue-uniformed policeman. The olive-skinned man's dark eyes quickly surveyed the room. He frowned when he saw Oriana and Flint. His expression became even more severe when his eyes alighted on the Barone, who was pouring himself another anisette.

"Excuse us for interrupting you, Contessa, but I'd like to speak in private to the Barone Casarotto-Re."

"May I ask what this intrusion is all about?"

"It's all right, Barbara. Whatever you have to say to me, Commissario, you can say in front of my friends."

Bobo must have intended it for a brave pose, but his voice, though haughty, had a hollow and fearful sound.

"Very well, then. I am Commissario Roberto Gemelli of the Venice Questura. We'd like you to come to San Lorenzo to answer some questions in reference to the deaths of Hugh Moss and Marie Quimper, who were shot to death last night in the Rialto Erberia."

Bobo paled.

"Dead? Both of them?"

"My God!" the Contessa said. "Moss called me about a quarter to twelve last night and was going to stop by. Now I see why he didn't! To think I've been in a pique about it!"

Gemelli was about to say something when Oriana said:

"It happened much too late for the paper! We went to the Flora to see if Hugh and Marie wanted to go to Chioggia. Hugh mentioned the Carpaccio there. And—"

Oriana broke off at a sharp look from Gemelli.

"You and Signor Flint will be giving your statements at the

Questura later, Signora Borelli. Please, Barone. Our boat is waiting."

"I'll never forgive you unless you do something to help Bobo!"

Urbino was fortified with a Campari soda, the Contessa only by an anger that didn't seem at all close to cooling. She had not very graciously asked Oriana and Flint to leave and then called the chief commissioner at the Questura to complain about the way Gemelli had taken away Bobo.

"I don't see what I can do, Barbara."

"Well, I do! Haven't I already started the ball rolling? You can help convince Gemelli that Bobo knows absolutely nothing about this couple!"

"Bobo will have to tell Gemelli what he does know about the couple. It might not be as little as you think."

"He knows even less about them than I do, and what I know can be put in one of those thimbles over there," she said, nodding to her collection of Victorian thimbles. "Oh, how could Oriana have brought this down on our heads! If it weren't for her, we'd never have met Moss and Quimper! And now every single one of my guests is going to be dragged over to San Lorenzo and grilled."

Urbino gave a nervous, involuntary smile at her unintentional pun. The name of the quarter where the Questura was located was also the name of the saint who had been martyred by grilling over an open fire.

"I don't find as much humor in all this as you do! Please, Urbino, do try to get over this adolescent animosity for Bobo. I need you to set things straight. First those threats, and now this new trouble. You saw the way Gemelli was treating Bobo! As if he had something to hide! Go to the Questura and see what you can do for him."

Urbino's mind quickly ran over Bobo's strange behavior last night, his bloodied scarf, and Moss's failure to turn up at the Ca' da Capo-Zendrini after his call. Could he have been looking for Bobo? But instead of coming to the Ca' da Capo, he had gone with Marie Quimper to the deserted Rialto Market, where they had met their deaths.

"You keep mentioning Oriana and your other guests," Urbino said, "but Gemelli is going to be very interested in Moss's call to you last night. That brings things even closer to you—and to Bobo."

"And to you as well!" she snapped. "Maybe he knew you were here and wanted to see *you!*"

"It was you, Barbara. You're going to have to start to face the truth."

When the Contessa responded after a few moments, she spoke with a regretful smile that warmed her gray eyes. Her anger of a moment before seemed forgotten.

"I pulled you away from the mud at Abano so that you could play one of your favorite roles, remember?—my knight in shining armor who comes to the rescue in your own quiet way. Don't disappoint me. With these deaths there's much more at stake than before." Then, in a quiet but insistent voice: "And beware of your dislike for Bobo. It shows, *caro*, oh, it shows!"

Several hours later at the Questura, Urbino gave his statement to Commissario Gemelli while a stenographer took it down. He described how he had met Moss and Quimper at Harry's Bar when Oriana and Flint had introduced them.

"Quimper asked me to autograph a copy of my book on Proust. She said that she had read it but a receipt from the Libreria Sangiorgio showed that she had just bought it that day, which suggests that the book itself might have been only a pretext for meeting me. Oriana Borelli and Flint met them at the exhibit at the Palazzo Grassi. Later that same day I bumped into them in Piazza San Marco. They were standing under the arcade outside the Chinese salon."

"Observing the Barone and the Contessa?"

"Perhaps. They were still sitting there. Moss asked me earlier at Harry's if the Contessa was with me."

He then described the comments about their *Baedeker*.

"Did you happen to look through it?"

"No. Quimper was nervous. Moss jumped in and said that it was very expensive. He interrupted her again when I asked if it was their first trip to Venice. He said it was but I had the impression Quimper had been about to say something else. The next time I saw them was that evening. The Barone and I were on the terrace of the Gritti Palace about ten. Moss and Quimper were being rowed into the gondola landing below the terrace. They looked up at me and exchanged a few words with each other. I waved. They returned my greeting."

"Perhaps they were interested in Casarotto-Re, or even in your relationship with him. After all, they had three encounters with you in one day, two of them touching on Casarotto-Re. And they were at his play and the Contessa's reception. Either they knew him or knew who he was."

"Moss didn't have a good opinion of the performance. Maybe he was jealous of the Barone. He was the jealous type. He snapped at Quimper when she said something about my jacket photograph, and Oriana mentioned how upset he became with her over Flint."

"There *is* something shifty in Flint—and I wouldn't be surprised if he's on some kind of drug or other. He *is* very good-looking, though. He could very easily have turned Quimper's head. She wasn't much of a looker, even before her face was smashed by a bullet. Was she flirtatious?"

"I never saw any sign of it, but who knows?"

He described the way Moss had been staring at the Barone at the Contessa's reception, his own encounter with the couple in the Contessa's garden, and Moss's behavior at the bookstore. Saving it for last, he then told Gemelli about Moss's midnight call to the Contessa.

"The Contessa thinks he might have wanted to do some painting at the Ca' da Capo-Zendrini."

"And I suppose she just thinks it's only a coincidence they were murdered?"

Gemelli got up and went to the window overlooking the canal. He stared absently down at the canal.

"If Moss was jealous, their deaths might have something to do with another man," he said. "But who? Casarotto-Re? He suggested that Moss shot Quimper, then himself. What he doesn't know—or maybe he does all too well—is that no gun was found near the bodies. In fact, no gun at all has been found. Casarotto-Re insists he never saw Moss and Quimper before he was introduced to them at the reception. He said nothing about seeing them in the gondola."

Gemelli turned from the window.

"Not much love seems to be lost between you and Casarotto-Re. It can't be any fun sitting on the sidelines and watching your Contessa gad about town with a man you find insufferable! Listen, Macintyre. I find him *antipatico*, too, but the difference between you and me is that you feel damned guilty about it. *I* take it as a sign he can't be trusted, that he's trying to prove he's smarter than me. He's hiding something—and he's afraid."

This closely approximated Urbino's own impressions, but he was perhaps more on his guard than Gemelli, who didn't seem sufficiently aware of the extent to which the Barone, being an actor, was in control of appearances. Like all gifted actors—and Urbino gave him this—you always had to ask yourself if what you were seeing and responding to was true or if it was a performance.

As Urbino silently went over what he had told Gemelli, it almost seemed a betrayal—or at least he knew it would be considered in this light by the Contessa. But surely the best way to help her—and also Bobo, if he was innocent—was to conceal nothing?

There was a low knock at the door. It was a young officer, who handed Gemelli a folder and left. Gemelli looked at several photographs in the folder, then read two typewritten sheets. He nodded his head, closed the folder, and laid it on his already cluttered desk. He dismissed the stenographer.

"We've had our differences in the past, Macintyre," he said. "But I'd like to think that we've come to a meeting of minds. You've been of help to me. I admit I've taken credit for what you've done. I would even say that you have some regard for me. Am I right?"

He didn't wait for Urbino to answer.

"We both want to find out if Casarotto-Re had anything to do with the deaths of these two people. There's no doubt it was homicide." He nodded down at the folder. "That's the preliminary medical report. Take a look at the photographs. You might find them interesting."

Urbino had seldom seen the face of violent death. A drowning victim dragged from the Grand Canal and a man with an almost humorously neat bullet hole in the middle of his broad forehead had so far been the extent of it. But these photographs were different. Marie Quimper's blankly staring eyes and twisted mouth foamed with blood were loud, mute testimonies to the horror and brutality of sudden violent death. Moss was worse, his face unrecognizable, a mass of blood, tissue, and bone. Urbino gave the photographs back to Gemelli.

"They were found in the storehouse area of the green market at half past midnight by a tourist who had lost her way. The man in charge of locking up is a bit lax and the gate into the compound was left open. They must have wandered in because of the fog the way the woman who found their bodies did—or they might have had a rendezvous. The place is full of hidden little areas and *cul de sacs* just perfect for a bit of sex or romance—or, in this case, murder.

"Moss was shot two times with a .32 Walther PPK automatic from a distance of three to five feet, one bullet piercing his heart, the other shattering his jaw. It's impossible that he shot Quimper first and then himself. And Quimper could never have shot him and then herself. She was shot once in the back with the same gun as she apparently tried to escape. Nasty. The medical examiner says they both died instantly, sometime around fifteen past midnight. It fits in with Moss's call to the Contessa at a quarter to midnight and the discovery of their bodies at half past. Two people in the area heard what they thought were firecrackers about ten or fifteen minutes past midnight. They didn't think anything of it because some pranksters have been setting them off recently. We'll know more in a couple of days. Do you want the person who did that"—he nodded grimly toward the photographs—"to get away with it?"

"Of course not," Urbino said, but he couldn't help but be wary of the Commissario's new spirit of cooperation.

"This time around, Macintyre, I'm going to share what I know with you," Gemelli said. "Those photographs are just the beginning. Between the two of us we'll have a much better chance of rooting out the bastard who did this. The very fact that you don't like Casarotto-Re will work to our mutual advantage. Given your obvious prejudice, I can be sure that whatever you come up with will be reliable. You'll be scrupulous."

Gemelli was giving him a way of reconciling his bias against the Barone with his promise to the Contessa.

"And if your own fair-mindedness fails you," Gemelli went on, "your regard for the Contessa da Capo-Zendrini won't,

one way or the other. You want to get at the truth behind
Casarotto-Re for her sake. *She* doesn't find him *antipatico* at
all. That's easy enough to see."

He picked up a crushed pack of cigarettes, extracted one,
and straightened it. He threw the pack back on the desk. He lit
the cigarette and stood smoking for several moments, leaning
against the filing cabinet behind him.

"It's not just my professional nose that scents something
wrong with our Barone, but what we found when we searched
Moss and Quimper's room at the Hotel Flora."

He picked a book up from his desk that Urbino hadn't noticed earlier because of all the clutter. Its red leather covers
were faded and frayed, its marbleized page edges stained in
various places. A thin, dark blue cloth bookmark, its end torn
and wispy, stuck out from the bottom of the book. On the
front cover in faint gold leaf lettering was *Baedeker's Northern
Italy*.

Gemelli handed the guidebook to Urbino.

"That's one of the things we found in the room. Turn to
page 363 in the section on Venice."

When Urbino did, he found several lines of text underlined
in red pencil:

> SALA DELLA BUSSOLA, antechamber of the three
> Inquisitors of the Republic (view into the courtyard
> of the Carceri, p. 367). On the exit-wall (the former
> entrance) is an opening, formerly adorned with a
> lion's head in marble, into the mouth of which
> (*Bocca di Leone*) secret denunciations were thrown.

Urbino riffled through the other pages of the book. He didn't
see any other underlined sections.

"We also found these," Gemelli said.

Urbino laid the *Baedeker* on the desk as Gemelli handed
him several sheets of red typewriter-sized paper. On each was
printed in Italian in block letters, word for word, the same

threat that had been placed in the *bocca di leone* at the Doges' Palace and sent to the *Gazzettino*.

"You see what all this means? Same paper. Same words. Same letters. Moss and Quimper—or maybe one of them— were circulating the threats against Casarotto-Re. When I showed him the book and these sheets, he said he had no idea the couple had been involved, but he knew all right, and he knew before the reception. He was being blackmailed. He wanted to put an end to it, but he wasn't happy about having the police—or you—involved."

"But couldn't those sheets have been planted in their room—and the passage underlined—by someone else?"

"And this same person killed Moss and Quimper? Or maybe someone *else* just came along and killed them? Usually the simplest explanation is the right one. The accusation could have been a warning. After all, it doesn't say very much, does it? It was probably meant to be provocative, a threat of what could—and would—follow if Casarotto-Re didn't pay up, and pay up big. *He* would know what he was being threatened with. The question is: What is it about him that the couple might have been murdered for? The British and French consulates are providing information about them. But it's essential to find out more about Casarotto-Re himself."

Gemelli took a last drag on his cigarette and snuffed it out in the stub-filled ashtray on his desk.

"He can't account for his time from ten forty-five when he left Festa at the Flora after they had a drink at Harry's until he returned to the Ca' da Capo-Zendrini two hours later. Claims he was walking by himself and got a nosebleed. We'll check his medical records to see if he has a history of them as he claims. We're hoping the gun will turn up, but if it was thrown in the Grand Canal or the lagoon there's little chance of that. Casarotto-Re has had more than twelve hours to conceal or destroy anything incriminating. He took almost all his things from the Gritti Palace to the Contessa's, and his suite has been completely cleaned, but technicians are going over it. Some of my men are looking through his room at the Ca' da Capo-Zendrini. That's where Casarotto-Re is now."

"You said he took almost everything from the Gritti Palace to the Contessa's. What didn't he take?"

"The suede jacket, scarf, and gloves he was wearing last night. He'd already given them to the Gritti cleaning service."

When Urbino got back to the Ca' da Capo-Zendrini, the Contessa was in the study dictating letters to Harriet with an abstracted look.

"Finally! I've been going mad. That'll be all, Harriet. I just can't concentrate. Don't forget to call the Municipality about the procession. They *must* allow it to begin at midnight. That was our agreement."

Harriet obviously hadn't got much sleep after her late night return from Zeoli's. Dark circles ringed her eyes. Uncomfortable under Urbino's scrutiny, she hurried from the room.

"Do you know what's been going on around here since you've left?" the Contessa asked in an accusatory tone.

"I know that some police officers came and searched Bobo's room. But he consented."

"Consented! As if he had much choice! And what about me! Two times in one day the police have—have invaded the Ca' da Capo!"

"Now, Barbara, aren't you being a bit melodramatic?"

The Contessa eased herself back into the chair in front of her escritoire.

"Melodramatic? Is that how you think of my pain? My outrage? Is that what it's come to?"

These words—and their histrionic delivery, complete with

round-eyed disbelief—were equally, if not even more, melodramatic than her previous exclamation.

"Where is Bobo?" Urbino asked as he sat down.

"Thank God not in some dank cell! He's resting. He went straight to his room. He didn't even have the energy to tell me what happened at the Questura. After what he's gone through even a man half his age would have collapsed. Neither of us has had time to eat a single bite."

She asked Lucia to bring some *tramezzini*. While they waited, she kept her silence with considerable noise, rearranging the papers and objects on her escritoire. After Lucia brought the tray, the Contessa selected one of the crustless sandwiches, but the next moment she put it down on her plate. Urbino picked up a Gorgonzola sandwich and started to eat it with considerable relish until he saw how the Contessa was watching him.

"I'm glad to see that you still have your appetite. Usually it's the opposite after you've seen Gemelli. Why the difference this time around?"

The Contessa's expression—concerned, slightly belligerent, but all the while also vulnerable—reminded him of how delicate his position was. Everything involving the Barone since Urbino had returned from his mud therapy had required tact and patience. The situation was much worse now.

"Gemelli seems to be in a new spirit of cooperation. We won't have to pull as many strings as we usually do. He's already shown me the medical examiner's report. Moss and Quimper were definitely murdered."

" 'A new spirit of cooperation.' How interesting! And what, may I ask, is his reason?"

"He wants my help. I was acquainted with Moss and Quimper and observed certain things about them—"

"And some of those things involve Bobo! That's it in a nutshell! I'm not that dull-witted! Between the two of you, you want to do him in! It's a conspiracy!"

"With that attitude you're going to do Bobo more harm

than good! Moss called you a short time before they were killed. You're involved yourself from Gemelli's point of view and don't think it doesn't give him satisfaction!"

"It doesn't matter a fig what he thinks of me! And Bobo had absolutely nothing to do with these murders! You're a fifth column, a Quisling, a—a—oh, what's your sad American equivalent? Yes!" she said forcefully. "A Benedict Arnold! Although *he* was a hero in *my* country."

For a moment the anger on the Contessa's face ebbed away into confusion—as well it should have, given the convoluted logic of her last words—but she recovered herself and nodded with satisfaction.

"Oh, how can I trust you? How can *we* trust you?"

She looked forlornly at the door as if seeking out the about-to-be-betrayed Barone, who just might have wandered down to find out what all the excitement was about.

"You *can* trust me, Barbara. But you're right. I don't like Bobo! I don't know if it's him or—or *you* and him. Even before he came into the picture I was out of sorts. I still am, with worries about this damn gout, silly and self-indulgent though it seems to you. Seeing you so wrapped up in Bobo makes everything even worse. I'm happy for you, but I don't want you hurt in any way. And I keep bumping up against the fact that I just don't trust him, and the crazy thing is that I don't have much faith in my own reaction either!"

"Why, you're jealous!" the Contessa said with an inappropriate but nonetheless big smile. "You sweet, dear, little man! I want to come over and give you a kiss!"

She didn't, but instead kept beaming as if at a mischievous child.

"So you see, Barbara, because I *am* aware of my bias, I'll do whatever I can to be absolutely fair."

This struck his own ears as more than a little smooth and facile, not to mention naive. The Contessa didn't look convinced.

"To show you how bad things are for Bobo, you should know

that copies of the threats were found in Moss and Quimper's room at the Flora as well as other evidence."

The Contessa was stunned.

"We have three possibilities, Barbara, and only three. One: Moss and Quimper were murdered for some unknown reason by someone who then planted those things in their room to implicate Bobo. Two: They were murdered by one person but the sheets and guidebook were left by someone else who wanted to take advantage of the murders to make trouble for Bobo. This person was blackmailing Bobo and underlined the pertinent passage in the guidebook. Three: Moss and Quimper were threatening Bobo, and they've been murdered because of it in some way. Don't delude yourself, Barbara. Bobo is involved— one way or another. The only question is how deeply."

"I'll leave you to contemplate the possibilities on your own. I'm going to put a cold compress on my face and rest. And please let Bobo restore himself before you start badgering him with questions. Stay here if you like, but make good use of your time by reconsidering some of your wild notions."

"Yes, two policemen came back here and went through my room," Bobo told Urbino in the *salotto blu* an hour later. "I told them they could turn everything upside down as long as they didn't cut the paintings from the frames or break the ceramic palm trees. Quite thorough, they were. They wanted to know what clothes I was wearing last night. I told them I gave my suede jacket, scarf, and gloves to the Gritti housekeeper. Then, when I said that Barbara's maid had already washed some of my other things, they acted as if I had imposed on the poor girl in the middle of the night. It *is* her job!"

Bobo ate one of the *tramezzini*, then emptied his wineglass. As Urbino filled their glasses from a bottle of Bardolino, he said: "You seem blasé about all this, but Gemelli is very serious. There *have* been two murders."

"I'm aware of that, but I can't make myself worry about it when I know I'm innocent, can I?"

"It would upset me very much if I were unjustly accused."

"As it would me, but I haven't been accused of anything," Bobo reminded him. "I could give a list of people who had as much contact with Moss and Quimper as I did." He raised his glass. "I'm a lamb, Urbino, a true and veritable lamb." After his sip he nodded as if in approval of either the Bardolino or his comment. "But although I might be a lamb I have no intention of being led to the slaughter—by anyone!"

"That means you'll make things as clear as possible about your relationship with Moss. It's the only way you can protect yourself."

"Be assured that I didn't have *any* relationship with him or the girl. That's what you—*we*—have to convince your friend the Commissario about. I never saw either of them before Barbara's reception."

The bold look he gave Urbino wavered. Fear was in the air. Whatever secret Bobo might be harboring, he was intelligent enough to realize that a murder investigation was bound to flush it out.

Urbino brought up the incident of Moss and Quimper in the gondola beneath the Gritti Palace terrace.

"I vaguely remember the couple in the gondola but I didn't realize it was them. To know they were involved with those threats baffles me. Has it occurred to you that the murderer could have planted them in their room to point a finger at me?"

"But if that's what happened, you have a *different* kind of problem—just as bad if not worse. It would mean that the person threatening you is also a murderer, someone who might have killed

Moss and Quimper for a reason related to you. If you're hiding anything, whether about them or someone else, no matter how trivial you think it may be, it would be better to mention it now rather than later—all the more so if you're innocent."

" 'Hiding anything,' you say?" Bobo gave a hollow laugh, showing rows of impossibly white teeth. "I've already told the Commissario everything."

"But you didn't mention that you had some words with Moss at your book signing, words that seemed to have something to do with Barbara."

"With Barbara? How preposterous!" Again the hollow laugh. "I don't remember what we said to each other. Which means it must have been of little consequence."

"That wasn't my impression."

"But that's the problem with impressions, isn't it? They're so often wrong."

"What did you and Livia do after the performance?" Urbino asked, abruptly switching his focus.

"We went to Harry's Bar to celebrate our success."

"How long were you there?"

"About half an hour—until ten-thirty."

"Not long for a celebration. What did you do then?"

"I walked Livia to the Flora and left. No, wait a minute. Before I left I called her on the house phone to remind her to look in on Orlando. I had forgotten to tell her."

The Flora was about a ten-minute walk from Harry's. Bobo had returned to the Ca' da Capo-Zendrini about twelve forty-five. Even a slow walk or the local vaporetto would have brought him back at least an hour earlier.

"Moss called Barbara about midnight. He wanted to drop by. Do you know anything about that?"

"Absolutely nothing. Why should I?"

"Moss and Quimper were staying at the Flora. You could have seen them when you walked Livia back. Moss could have told you he was thinking of coming here."

Bobo stared icily at Urbino.

"I didn't see Moss after the reception. I was only at the Flora a short time. We said good night and I made my way back here on foot. I got lost and ended up on the embankment across from the cemetery island."

This surprised Urbino. Although it was easy to get lost in Venice, it was unusual to go this far astray making your way to a palazzo on the Grand Canal.

"And your nosebleed?"

"Oh, that! I lost my footing going up a bridge. I didn't hit my nose but the jarring provoked the nosebleed. I'm very sensitive when it comes to them."

"Are you sure you didn't walk through the Rialto Market when you were lost?"

"Absolutely not!" Then, with what must have been intended as a no-nonsense expression, he added: "Know this and know this well, Urbino: I want the murderer found as soon as possible. And not only because of how bad it looks for me. This person is crazed! Who knows which of us might be struck down next?" When he took a sip, his hand was visibly shaking. "Just knowing that someone other than that bumbling Commissario is looking into things will be a comfort. Barbara says that he's asked you to help. Just watch out for his tricks! I give you a *carte blanche* to talk to whomever you like. I have nothing to hide. You'll find me the soul of understanding and patience. After all, we both have the same end in mind, don't we?"

After Urbino left, Bobo called the Hotel Flora from his bedroom. Disguising his voice on the off chance that it might be recognized, he asked for Livia Festa's room. He waited impatiently as the phone rang. He was about to give up when Festa answered.

Bobo spoke in low, urgent tones. Someone right outside his door would have been unable to hear anything he said until, near the end of the conversation, he raised his voice and said angrily: "Unless you want everything to come out, you'll keep your mouth shut! Remember: I called you after we said good night. We talked for one or two minutes. I reminded you to check to see how Orlando was doing." Bobo listened to her response then said: "You don't need to know. Just don't forget what I said. And we haven't had this conversation. In fact, we haven't spoken to each other since last night."

Bobo hung up and wondered if there was anything he had forgotten.

The next morning at Florian's, Urbino took the *Gazzettino* from the rack and ordered a *caffelatte*. A piece on the murders told him nothing new. No mention was made of the threats against the Barone or the items found in the couple's room.

Urbino stared out into Piazza San Marco and thought about various aspects of the case. The swiftness with which Bobo had had his clothes cleaned by the Gritti housekeeper and the Contessa's maid was puzzling. Did it say anything more than that Bobo was fastidious?

Then there was Bobo's casual dismissal of his encounter with Moss at the book signing. Why had Moss come unless for a compelling reason? Of course, a threat had been left. Perhaps that was reason enough for Moss and Quimper's presence, but somehow Urbino doubted it. And anyone at the signing could have left the threat.

On the short walk to the Hotel Flora, Urbino saw the Contessa. She was coming out of the Banca Commerciale Italiana. She had a strained look on her face and grasped her Gucci bag tightly under her arm. When she saw Urbino, she started.

"Urbino! You shouldn't creep up on people like that! What are you doing here?" Since "here" was the heart of Venice, she must have realized the strangeness of her question and quickly said: "Up early as usual, I see. I hope it's to make efforts on Bobo's behalf." She paused, looked uncomfortable. "Well, I have to be going. I'm on my way to Venetia Studium," she said, naming the shop that sold hand-printed fabrics and items done in the Fortuny "*plissé*" technique.

She hurried off. Urbino watched her until she darted into the shop.

"Mademoiselle Quimper was nice enough but her friend was impossible!" the manager at the Hotel Flora said. "Always complaining—about the room, our rates, the breakfast, noise from the garden, everything! He had a chip on his shoulder. Very quick to anger—but don't misunderstand me. No one deserves to die like that. My brother-in-law in the police gave me all the details."

"Did Moss or Quimper make any telephone calls from their room on the evening they were murdered?"

"No—and they didn't get any either. I was on the desk. It's not my shift, but one of the staff got sick."

"I'm sure you've gone through it all with the police but would you mind telling me if you noticed anything unusual that night?"

"Not really, but, well," he said hesitantly, "there *was* something about the Barone Casarotto-Re. I didn't tell the police because I forgot it at the time. My brother-in-law told me this morning that they found something in the couple's room that indicated they might not have liked the Barone."

If Gemelli found out that one of his men was giving away vital information in a murder investigation, he would be furious. Urbino had to go cautiously.

"I don't know anything about that," he said.

"Neither do I," the manager said quickly, "but you asked if I noticed anything unusual the night of the murder, and the Barone came here about ten forty-five with Signora Festa. He made a call on the house telephone."

He nodded toward the small adjacent room.

"Do you know which room he called?"

"More's the pity," the manager said regretfully. "It was a few minutes after Signora Festa went up in the elevator. He talked for a few minutes and then left. Moss and his friend went out together about five minutes later. That was the last time I saw them. About ten minutes later Signora Festa came down with her dog."

"Did you notice when she returned?"

"No."

Urbino thanked him and rang Orlando Gava's room on the house phone. Gava told him to come up. He came to the door in a black jacket. The black armband was still in place. His homely face with its pendulous lower lip was freighted with sadness. He led Urbino to a room furnished in antiques that overlooked the garden. Gava sat on the sofa next to scattered copies of *Gente, Oggi,* the *Gazzettino,* and the Rome and Milan papers. On a little table were several portrait photographs in elaborate frames and a flickering votive candle. Next to them was a small plastic aerosol inhaler. Urbino sat in an armchair, after removing from its cushions a worn leather book with protruding leather alphabet tabs.

"How are you feeling, Signor Gava?"

"Well enough. Asthma. It runs in the Gava family. An attack can come on in seconds," he said gravely, nodding his head. "This room is filled with little things that could start me going before I could even say my prayers!" He cast an oddly fluttering eye around the room as if accessing its deadly possibilities. "Dust, the smoke in the drapes, even the newsprint! I guess I'm lucky—so far. Not like Rosa. All alone, and only forty-six. Exactly ten years ago. It puts me in such a state that I wish—"

He didn't express his dark wish but fixed his eyes now on the photographs. Urbino remembered how he had said "I'm coming, Rosa" before passing out for a second time.

"Well, you're not alone, Signora Gava. You have Livia Festa looking in on you."

"Looking in on me? Where did you get that idea? Who wants her and her dog poking their noses around here?"

"You've heard about the young couple who were murdered, haven't you? They were staying here. You might have met them at the Contessa's reception."

"Before that, here at the hotel. Barely a nod and a *buon giorno* at first, but the man became a lot friendlier once he saw Bobo and me together. Everyone notices him. An actor down to his fingertips! It'll be that way until he's made his last exit."

He gauged Urbino's response with furtive glances from his bloodshot eyes.

"When did the man start being more friendly?"

"A few days before the Contessa's reception. Bobo and I were at the hotel bar. The young man came in with his sweet little girlfriend. He kept staring at us and said something to her. She looked nervous, but she always looked nervous, like a bird waiting for a snake to gobble her up, poor thing. He would shake his finger at her during breakfast and she wouldn't say a word. A saint. She reminded me of my sister. But I was telling you about Bobo and the young man, wasn't I? Well, that evening the young man came over to me when Bobo left and—"

Gava stopped abruptly as if something had just struck him

and stared at Urbino, his pendulous lower lip more flaccid than usual, the sunlight from the windows glancing off his bald head. Once again, as he had been at the thermal spa, Urbino was reminded of the caricature of a corrupt Roman senator from the time of the Caesars.

"What did he say?"

Gava nodded his large head slowly.

"You're very curious about him, aren't you? Does it have something to do with what Livia said is your interest in solving crimes—like those threats against Bobo?"

"A commissario at the Venice Questura has asked me to help the police in whatever way I can."

"I've already told them what I know," Gava said warily.

"I'm sure you have, but if you wouldn't mind indulging me, it might help your brother-in-law."

Urbino wasn't sure whether this inducement would loosen or tighten Gava's tongue.

"Of course I want to help Bobo," Gava said quickly. "Let me see. What was it exactly that the young man said? Something like, 'I see that you know the Barone Casarotto-Re. My friend and I are admirers of his.' Only then did he introduce himself. His Italian wasn't good so I answered in English. I introduced myself and said that the Barone was my brother-in-law. He sort of brightened up when I said my name, wanted to know if my sister, the Barone Casarotto-Re's wife, was in Venice, too. I said she had been dead for ten years. But when he started to say how sad it was to have her die so young—and maybe so suddenly—and how difficult it probably had been for the Barone, I excused myself and left. None of his business!"

Urbino asked if he had ever told Moss that Bobo had been married to his sister.

"I only said he was my brother-in-law."

Urbino thought for a few moments. Just because Bobo was Gava's brother-in-law didn't automatically mean he had to be married to his sister. Gava's brother or sister could have married one of Bobo's siblings. Any of these combinations would have made them brothers-in-law. Italians usually didn't make fine distinctions in the question of in-laws. But Moss seemed to have known that Gava and the Barone were brothers-in-law because the Barone had married his sister. That may be why he recognized Gava's name—because of Gava's sister.

"Perhaps someone could have told him that Bobo had married a Gava," Urbino said, "and might have pointed you out as the brother-in-law."

"But he gave no indication that he knew who I was before he saw me with Bobo. It was Bobo who made the difference," he said adamantly.

"Has your sister's maiden name been mentioned recently in articles on Bobo?"

"Not that I know of. If it has, it wasn't because he wanted to have Rosa remembered!" Gava said angrily. "He's hardly given her a thought since she died, unless he was thinking about the money she left him."

"What exactly happened to her?"

"She was an asthmatic, as I said, and was dependent on her inhaler. She had an attack when she was alone one night. It seems she had no medication left. She lost consciousness and went into a coma. She never recovered. I almost died myself from grief. And from guilt."

"But why should you feel guilty?"

"Because I was out enjoying myself with Bobo and Livia! Eating at one of the most expensive restaurants in Taormina. Not that I wanted to go but those two convinced me, said that Rosa would be fine for a few hours. She even encouraged me to go herself, but that was because she saw how much the others wanted it. Every year, when her anniversary comes around as it is now, I—I—" He shook his head slowly and when he looked at Urbino his eyes held a deep, dark sorrow. "This is my Rosa."

Gava took one of the photographs from the table and handed it to Urbino. It was a three-quarter photograph of a sweet-faced woman about forty, dressed in black with a string of pearls. She had fair hair, simply dressed, and wore a tentative smile. The main resemblance to her brother was her sad eyes and a general air of ill health.

"*Simpatica*," Urbino said, handing the photograph back.

"*Moltissimo!*" Gava kissed the photograph and put it back with the others. "These are my beloved dead: Rosa, our mother and father, our grandparents, our mother's sister—my god-mother. They go with me everywhere. They're my portable graveyard," he said with a smile that only added more sorrow to his face. "Who will remember me, I wonder? The only immortality we have is in the mind of the living! Don't forget it, young man! Someone will come along and throw all these away, be sure of it! And that day will be here soon! Very soon!" he said darkly, once again his eyes straying to Rosa's photograph.

"How did Bobo take your sister's death?"

Gava's head snapped up.

"I thought you were interested in the young couple! Why do you want to know about Rosa and Bobo?"

"You brought them up yourself, Signor Gava."

"You can be just as slippery as Bobo! He told me that I would have to be careful with you. I see he was right."

"When did Bobo mention me? Did he call you the night the couple was murdered?"

"There you go again! Questions instead of answers! I can see why Bobo is afraid of you. Yes, afraid! No, he didn't call me that night. Last night, to warn me that you'd be asking questions. *I* have nothing to be afraid of! But Bobo is scared silly of being associated with these murders. With good reason, too! First he gets those threats. Then this young man shows an interest in him and is murdered with his girlfriend. And today Bobo tells me that you might be asking questions about him and I should be careful of what I said. Oh yes, Bobo is afraid! He's not good enough an actor to hide *that*!"

Did Gava know something incriminating about Bobo? Gava,

he had said, knew more about his life than he did himself. What power might it give the sickly man? Was he the type to abuse the power? He had been very quick to deny any role in the threats made against Bobo, but he had expressed his dislike of D'Annunzio at the reception, a dislike echoed in the threats.

"If you want to know more about the poor couple, ask Livia. She knows them from somewhere. She knows a lot about people. A crafty, devious woman! I wonder how she'd feel about someone knowing a lot about *her*?"

The possibility didn't seem to strike Gava as amusing, but quite the opposite.

Urbino and Festa took their drinks from the bar into the sun-washed garden of the flora. The weather had returned to goldenness but the crispness of the air was like a reminder of mortality. Peppino was nosing among the potted hydrangeas under the indulgent eye of his mistress. Festa, dressed in colors she informed Urbino were "eggplant" and "malachite," rattled on nervously about her seamstress of the past twenty-three years.

"She made a matching coat for Peppino but it's too warm for him with the lovely weather we've been having."

Peppino, hearing his name, jumped on her lap.

"It does get chilly at night, though. You must put it on him when you take him for a walk at night."

"Of course, but listen to us chatting about Peppino as if he's the most important person around! It will turn his little head!" She paused and considered this part of Peppino's anatomy for a few moments, then said, in an offhand manner: "Now that *Pomegranate* has finished its run here, I suppose we won't be seeing any more threats against Bobo."

"Then you think they had to do with the show?"

"With the show and with D'Annunzio, yes. What else? If they had received any publicity, I would almost have been glad for them. There would have been a bigger box office. D'Annunzio always thrived on notoriety."

"And Bobo?"

Festa smiled. She must once have been voluptuous, with the kind of full body that, no matter what the vogue, never really goes out of style as far as most men are concerned. The way she draped herself in loose-fitting garments surely was intended not only to conceal but also to free the imagination of susceptible men. Bobo had his susceptibilities, it seemed, since he had almost married her at some time in the past, according to Gava.

"Bobo only likes *good* publicity."

"Surely good publicity could be defined as any kind that brings in more money."

"Not where he's concerned. He cares what people think. His good reputation is his fortune. He doesn't have Barbara's or Oriana Borelli's kind of money. Not by a long shot! Never did."

"Have you spoken with him since yesterday?"

"Not since closing night. We had a drink at Harry's after the performance and then he walked me to the Flora. He called me on the house phone after we said good night. He wanted me to look in on Orlando. He had forgotten to mention it."

Almost the same words as Bobo had used.

"And did you?"

Festa reddened.

"I'm afraid not. I—I forgot all about it."

"But you did walk Peppino, I understand. Do you know about the murders of the young couple?"

"Of course. It's the talk of the hotel. So it seems you've switched your sleuthing from the threats against Bobo to the murders."

Festa's voice held a note Urbino couldn't identify.

"The Questura thinks they might be related."

99

"And why is that?"

If it was true that she and Bobo hadn't spoken since the murders, she wouldn't know about the threats and the *Baedeker* found in Moss and Quimper's room. He told her now, mainly to assess her reaction.

"My God! How terrible for Bobo! The very people murdered who might have been threatening him! I must call him at once."

But she didn't get up. Urbino wished she had, for he wondered where she would have tried to contact the Barone. At the Gritti Palace or the Ca' da Capo-Zendrini, where she had no way of knowing he had been since last night?

"He and Barbara must be out and about somewhere. They really seem to be making the circuits, don't they? Leaves you with a lot of time on your hands. You should be able to solve this case in no time." There was no mistaking Festa's tone now. It was pointed and snide. "Well, I'm not surprised," she went on coolly. "About the threats originating with Moss, I mean. We can understand what he had against Bobo. The girl must just have been along for the ride. But how absurd for the police to think Bobo had anything to do with the murders!"

"What do you think Moss had against Bobo?"

"He was jealous!" She stared at Urbino as if he were a dunce. "Is it so hard to believe that a man in his twenties could be jealous of a man more than twice his age? Bobo is very appealing. His age and experience only make him more so. You can be sure that many men would like to be exactly like him. I don't mean to suggest that Bobo gave Moss any *reason* to be jealous. The little French girl wasn't his type, for one thing!"

"Gava said she reminded him of his sister Rosa."

Festa raised an eyebrow that was more pencil than hair.

"Did he now? I knew Rosa. Nothing like the French girl, but brothers see their sisters differently than everyone else, especially *Italian* brothers," she emphasized. "And Orlando refuses to let go after all these years. He's trying to—to immortalize her!"

Urbino remembered the touch of irritation in Festa's behavior the night of the Contessa's reception when Gava had reached out to touch his black armband. There didn't seem much love lost between Gava and Festa.

"He said that you knew the couple from somewhere."

"He's exaggerating as usual. I think he's going senile! I saw them once before the reception. In Florence at Madova's."

Madova's was a fashionable glove shop near the Ponte Vecchio. Urbino usually went there twice a year with her, buying one pair of gloves to her half dozen.

"I didn't know who they were at the time. Madova's has men clerks, who take the most wonderful care to be sure your gloves fit properly," she began.

Urbino nodded. The Contessa would place her elbow down on the counter, her hand standing upright, and the clerk would pull on a glove, inserting his fingers between each of hers in a smooth, practiced motion. It was a ritual that seemed to put the Contessa—and other women clients—in a flush of good spirits.

"The clerk was being very attentive to Marie Quimper. He had just put a glove on her, seeing that it fit properly, when Moss slapped his hand away and pulled off the glove roughly. I don't know if he was more angry at Quimper or the clerk. He looked like he was about to pick up the *allargaguanti* and poke their eyes out!"

The *allargaguanti* was the wooden glove stretcher that Madova kept on its counter.

"He had a crazed look in his eye. He dragged the poor girl from the shop before she knew what was happening. Neither of them recognized me at the reception and of course I didn't say a word. So you can understand why I'm not surprised that this Moss was making threats against Bobo. That encounter showed how volatile he was."

"Did you notice anything at all about the couple at the reception that might be important? Any words they had with each other"—Urbino was thinking about the raised voices in the garden—"or with anyone else?"

"Nothing at all. I hardly paid them any attention."

She stood up and rearranged Peppino in her arms.

"Surely you realize the utter ridiculousness of Bobo being in any way involved in those murders! Look for someone with a grudge against Moss, someone he might have pushed around because of his jealousy. Don't place any importance on those things found in the couple's room."

Festa swept off in her eggplant and malachite with Peppino cradled in her arms and went up to her room.

Before leaving the hotel, Urbino asked the manager if he had seen Gava coming in or going out on the night of the murders.

"I haven't seen him out at night at all since his attack, just in the morning. To get his papers and take his coffee at Caffè Quadri. But he's certainly spry for a man his age. I pray God I'll be the same."

"We met them completely by accident, didn't we, John dear?" Oriana said from a chair that looked like a slingshot. Urbino and Flint were sharing the neo-Biedermeier sofa, which gave a view through ceiling-high windows of the Basilica and the Doges' Palace across the sparkling blue expanse of the lagoon. Urbino had come directly to the Ca' Borelli after talking to Festa.

"Completely," Flint agreed. "At the exhibit at the Grassi Palace a week before the opening of *Pomegranate*."

"Why do you link it with the Barone's play?"

"Come now, Urbino," Oriana said with a laugh. "John is just

using Bobo's opening as a point of reference. If you want the actual date I can look it up in my diary."

She smiled coyly and pushed her sunglasses higher up on the bridge of her nose. The only place where Oriana's affectation of wearing sunglasses indoors seemed to make any sense was in her own living room. There was so much chrome, unadorned white walls, and bright light that Urbino sometimes wished he were wearing a pair himself.

"Oriana always takes her diary along with her so that she has something titillating to read," Flint said in his drawl.

Urbino didn't draw attention to the lack of originality in the observation but asked them what their accidental meeting with Moss and Quimper had been like.

Oriana said: "Marie—we didn't know her name at the time, of course—came up to us and asked in the sweetest *italiano* if we knew where she could find the carving shown on the cover of the catalogue. I said to myself, 'Now, if *she* isn't the image of that *americana* who turned the head of the Duke of Windsor and made him give up the crown!' What a love story! But none of her push and personality. Hugh came over a few moments later and we all introduced ourselves."

"Bobo wasn't with you by any chance, was he?"

"Of course not! We would have said if he had been! I'm not even sure if Bobo had come here yet."

"He had," Flint clarified. "Don't you remember? Barbara introduced us at Florian's the afternoon before."

"Introduced *you*, dear! I've known Bobo for almost as long as Barbara. But yes, you're right. I remember asking Barbara and Bobo if they wanted to come to the exhibit with us, but they couldn't. They had something else planned. I believe you were at Abano."

"You must have become friendly with them quickly," Urbino said.

"Oh, you know me! The essence of congeniality! We chatted

and looked at some of the exhibits together. John gave us the benefits of his expertise. Then it was lunchtime and I invited them to join us at the Montin."

"Did either of them bring up Bobo at any time?"

"No, but *I* did. I told them about the performance. Hugh had read quite a bit of D'Annunzio. I found it strange. God, who reads D'Annunzio these days! But don't tell Bobo I said so. I said that a friend was having a reception after opening night and why didn't they come?"

"Did you mention Barbara's name?"

"Name *and* title! Marie was impressed. She was such a sweetheart, poor little thing."

"And Moss?"

Oriana frowned.

"Very jealous. I mentioned at Barbara's reception how upset he got when Marie asked to see photographs of John."

"What were your impressions?" Urbino asked Flint.

"The same. I felt sorry for Marie. When the person you're with is jealous, it's hell for you."

"It's hell for the jealous person, too, John dear, but you wouldn't know about that, would you? I'm sure you've always been the object—or the cause—of jealousy."

Flint was wise enough not to respond to this. Instead he said: "Their murders must have had something to do with Hugh's jealousy."

"You had plans to go to Chioggia with them the morning after they were murdered," Urbino prompted.

"Not plans," Oriana said. "But when I suggested going to Chioggia that morning, John said it would be a nice gesture to see if they would like to go, too. He remembered how Hugh had mentioned the Carpaccio at the church there. I don't remember myself, but art is John's domain," she said loftily and with a mischievous smile suggesting what her own domain was. "And John spent more time with them than I did. He took them under his wing, showing them some of the sights. But tell us! All these questions about poor Hugh and Marie! You think there's some relationship between the threats and the murders, don't you? I can see it in your face! *Dio mio!* Poor Barbara! If she knows, she must be absolutely mad—*assoluta-mente!* Excuse me."

Oriana bounded up.

"I have to call her. Why don't you two take the boat to your apartment, John? You said you wanted to go back to your place for a few hours anyway. You can show Urbino what we found in Chioggia and get his opinion. I have to look after Barbara, *la poverina!*"

Flint had a small ground-floor apartment in San Polo, a few minutes walk from the Rialto. It was a furnished apartment, most of the pieces dark, heavy, and worn. But scattered among them were Flint's own belongings, which he proudly pointed out: a round table with mythological scenes of Wedgwood porcelain, several rococo Brustolon items, and a portrait by Lorenzo Lotto. It was none of these that Oriana had referred to, however, but a small bronze, finely designed and crafted.

"Tullio Lombardo, I'd say," Urbino said, examining it.

Flint's face lit up.

"That's what I thought! We found it in a shop in Chioggia."

They spent a few minutes chatting about the pleasures and surprises of stumbling on items like the bronze. Urbino got up and went to the window. It looked down on a typical Venetian scene—a small square with a covered wellhead carved with grotesque figures. Several obligatory cats sunned themselves and two old women in black were standing with shopping bags, their scarfed heads bent toward each other in intimate conversation.

"I like San Polo," Urbino said. "It has some of the best wine shops and restaurants. There's the Frari and San Rocco and," he added after a brief pause, "the Rialto markets. Do you shop there?"

"I eat in restaurants. My kitchen is bare." Flint said, his head bent over the bronze. "Wait until Oriana hears it's a real Tullio Lombardo!"

The phone rang. Flint jumped and picked it up. As he listened, his face was pinched with fear. After a few moments he put the receiver back in its cradle. He hadn't said a word.

"Bad news?"

"A wrong number. Just someone jabbering away in Venetian dialect."

His face was drained of color. He looked down quickly at his Piaget watch.

"That happens to me a lot, too. By the way, you say you found the bronze in Chioggia." Flint seemed to become more at ease at this apparent return to the topic of the bronze, but his jaw tensed when Urbino went on: "Moss mentioned the Carpaccio in Chioggia to you. I suppose the two of you talked about art quite a bit. What kind of art did he like?"

After a long pause, Flint said vaguely: "Modern art," then, with more enthusiasm and an exaggerated drawl: "Severini, Balla, Magritte, Malevich, Tanguy, Dalí."

There was an air of improvisation in the list. It was as if Flint was pulling the names from the Peggy Guggenheim catalogue.

"Somehow they don't quite suit the impression he made on me, but then you did know him better."

"I wouldn't say that! He wasn't much of a talker. As for Marie, I don't think I exchanged more than two or three words alone with her. Moss made sure of that."

Flint turned his face more directly toward Urbino, as if to illustrate exactly what the cause of Moss's jealousy had been.

The traces of age did little to detract from its appeal. Urbino wondered why he had changed careers.

When Flint stole another look at his watch, Urbino left.

Bobo surveyed the *calle*. It was empty. It was a good thing he had made a dry run earlier because he would have had trouble finding it, even with the directions, even with his map. Surely he wasn't far from a little square he sometimes visited, one with a D'Annunzio plaque lamenting the atrocities of war. But he had never wandered into this area of flaking, boarded-up buildings, where the gray, damp air penetrated to his bones.

He grasped the package more tightly. He was rather surprised at how small it was, considering what was in it. But maybe it wasn't so much what it contained that made the contrast with its smallness, but what its contents meant to him. And that was just about everything. Two people had already died—two stupid, infinitely selfish people who had wanted to bring down his fine scheme. But the nightmare hadn't ended, not even with their deaths. It was going on and on, and he was worse off than he had been before. He was in even greater danger now.

With both of them dead, he had felt a momentary sense of relief, but out there, he soon realized, was someone who knew. Who knew everything and had already shown how far he—or she—was willing to go.

When all this was over, he'd see that Urbino was put in his proper place. He knew he could do it with a minimum of effort. The Contessa would be his instrument. This gave him immense satisfaction and, full of nervous energy, he had to restrain a laugh.

He found the building, reached up and pried loose the

warped board. There was just enough room to push the package in. He heard it drop down onto the window ledge.

He turned around and left as quickly as he could. Since he had decided to do this, he would do it the right way, the way that would make things best for him. He was determined to succeed.

In a few minutes he was back in the thick of things, surrounded by people with their petty concerns.

The next morning, Urbino found the Contessa in the *salotto blu*. She was looking at a diagram of her bridge of boats that would span the lagoon from Venice to the cemetery island.

Urbino asked her if she had found what she wanted at Venetia Studium yesterday.

"Venetia Studium? Whatever do you mean? I—" Then she caught herself. "Oh, of course. No, there was nothing there that caught my fancy."

She studied the diagram as if she wanted to memorize it and then made a comment on the diversion of the water traffic around the bridge. Urbino asked if she would help find out more about Flint.

"Don't tell me you want to poke around in *his* affairs?" She put aside the diagram. "Whatever would that be in aid of? Oriana would be furious if she knew about it."

"We can't care what Oriana will think, Barbara. I need to know more about Flint."

"You're barking up the wrong tree but I'll see what I can do. I'll call Laura." Laura was her friend who worked in the fashion industry in Milan. "Any information you get is going to benefit Bobo. He's innocent, innocent, innocent! Of *everything* and *anything*! The world he's had to trudge through lately is thick with corruption and deceit, but not one atom will cling to him!"

"I can understand you championing him, Barbara. You're a loyal woman, but I don't want you to end up hurt. You're becoming very fond of Bobo."

"*Too* fond, is that what you mean? And why shouldn't I be? Doesn't he deserve it?" The Contessa raised her little chin. "He compliments me. He makes me feel ten times more alive. When we're not together, I have the strangest ache!" She looked at him with eyes in which surprise was almost keener than the softness one would expect to find, given her words. "Oh, you don't have to say it! I know it as clearly as I know my evening prayer! I'm a walking, breathing cliché! But I can't help it!" She paused for a beat. "I don't *want* to help it—and don't tell me that I must!"

"But if it's confusing your judgment, Barbara! If it's setting you up for a great fall or worse, I can't just stand around and say nothing! You can't expect that! I'm going through a lot myself! Don't forget that we have a very special relationship. That we—"

Urbino was almost glad when Harriet's entrance interrupted him. He was angry and he was hurt, and he was afraid where these feelings were leading him.

The Contessa, however, was seeing a new side to him that she didn't find at all disagreeable. She regretted the interruption and hoped that Urbino wouldn't lose his fervor, even if he said things she didn't like to hear.

With different moods, therefore, Urbino and the Contessa turned their attention to Harriet. The woman looked even more careworn than yesterday. If this was the result of a diet of natural foods, the avoidance of nightshades, and the suffering of periodic liver injections, then the woman should quickly seek out a completely new regimen—and perhaps a medical adviser other than Zeoli.

"This came for you today," she said in a dull, troubled voice, handing the Contessa a postcard. "I thought you'd want to see it immediately. I read it. I'm sorry, but it was almost automatic."

The Contessa looked at the front of the postcard, then turned it over. She spent several moments reading the back before handing it to Urbino with a frown.

The card showed a woman on a gurney. Her body was smeared with grayish mud. Behind the woman was a tiled wall with spigots and a hose. Standing over her, holding a metal bucket and wearing a smock, was a smiling, middle-aged woman. Printed in ink in English beneath the name of Zeoli's spa was: "Why not ask the Barone Casarotto-Re about Helen Creel? If he won't tell you, the therapist on the front of this card will. A concerned friend." The printing seemed identical to that on the threats.

"This is marvelous!" the Contessa exclaimed. "Bobo is off the hook! Moss and Quimper are dead and he's still getting threats—or whatever you want to call this trash!"

"It's postmarked the day of their murder," Urbino pointed out. "Does the name Helen Creel mean anything to you?"

"Absolutely nothing! And not to Bobo either, I'm sure!" She looked up at Harriet. "Thank you, Harriet dear. If anything else like this arrives I want to see it at once. By the way, are you still leaving this evening?"

"Yes, Barbara. I hope you understand."

"I want you to be happy, dear."

When Harriet left, the Contessa explained: "Harriet has decided to take an apartment. A dismal place in the Ghetto. Perhaps it's for the best, though. She's become difficult."

"In what way?"

"Mistakes, forgetting or misplacing things, but it's more than that." She gave Urbino a quick look. "Not to put too fine a point on it, I'm sure she's in love with Bobo. She acts so nervous around him, stealing glances, fidgeting when he looks at her. And she always seems in a daze. Yes, she's in love with Bobo!"

"Obviously it *has* to be Bobo," Urbino said with irritation, "since we all know he's so irresistible! But even before he graced us with his magnetic presence, Harriet was sprucing herself up. *I* say it's Zeoli."

The Contessa gave a little laugh, more an expression of delight in Urbino's reaction than in what he had said about Harriet and Zeoli.

"The relationship made in heaven? But I still say she's finding it too painful to be around Bobo now that he's staying here himself. But whether it's Bobo or Zeoli, I won't be completely sad to see her go."

"I remember how happy you were to have her staying here before Bobo came on the scene!"

"So I was." She looked down at the postcard. "But I'm surprised at us, Urbino! What kind of sleuths are we? We must get a plastic bag to put the postcard in."

This had barely been accomplished when Bobo and Zeoli came into the *salotto*. Urbino quickly slipped the postcard into his pocket.

Five minutes later, Urbino and Bobo were alone in the morning room. The Contessa was entertaining Zeoli, who had come to collect her donation to the health spa.

The two men sat across from each other in armchairs covered in Fortuny fabric. Bobo, dressed in fawn-colored corduroy trousers, crossed one long leg over the other and regarded Urbino with a barely perceptible smile.

"Let's not waste our time, Bobo. The chances of the threats

having been planted in Moss and Quimper's room are minimal. I'll be the first to apologize if it turns out they were. But you should wake up to the fact that you're about to be pulled in for something more serious than questioning. I'd like to help you."

"Indeed? How noble of you."

"There's no need to be so snide, Bobo. I want to tell you what I learned from Orlando."

When he finished, Bobo said: "I called him this morning. He wasn't all that coherent. He even tends to hallucinate when he's had one of these asthma attacks. Something to do with his medication."

"Did it have the same effect on your wife? She was an asthmatic, too. These susceptibilities often run in families. Like your nosebleeds."

Bobo said coldly: "I've often thought Orlando developed asthma out of sympathy with Rosa. He was so devoted to her. But certainly neither Rosa nor her condition can be pertinent to your inquiries."

"That remains to be seen." Urbino reached into his pocket and took out the postcard. "And what about this?"

Bobo's first response, when he saw the plastic envelope, was to say: "How antiseptic!" but then a flicker of fear crossed his handsome face. His hand shook as he took the postcard and turned it over. By the time he had read the back, he had himself under control.

"Who is Helen Creel?" Urbino asked.

"The name means nothing to me! What the hell is going on! It was bad enough when this—this trash was directed only against me. But Barbara! I won't stand for it!"

And Bobo went on and on in a theatrical display of outrage. Urbino let it run its course before saying: "So you have no idea why it mentions you in reference to a woman named Helen Creel?"

"None at all!" He jumped to his feet. "But Marco Zeoli is

with Barbara now! This is *his* thermal spa, isn't it? You don't think there's some connection? I mean about his coming just when the card was delivered?"

Urbino followed him to the *salotto blu*, where the Contessa was alone. Zeoli had just left. Before Bobo could do or say anything, Urbino excused himself and went after Zeoli.

Even out on the stern of the vaporetto in the crisp air Urbino kept catching whiffs of the mephitic odor that always seemed to cling to Zeoli. He could no more escape it than he could the unwelcome assault of Zeoli's account of the ravages of serious, untreated gout, all the details of which Zeoli seemed determined to give him without interruption.

Zeoli looked everywhere—at the facades of the palazzi, the boats, the gray waters, the embankments, the cloud-filled sky, the screaming seabirds—everywhere but at Urbino. As they approached the Rialto Bridge, his eyes didn't even flicker in the direction of the vegetable market. The pace of his professional flow quickened.

Urbino endured it for as long as he could. When Zeoli was catching his breath, Urbino said quickly:

"You may be in a position to help Barbara and me—and also the Barone. She received this in today's mail. It's a postcard of your treatment center."

Urbino took it from his pocket and handed it to him. Zeoli gave the front only a glance before turning it over. His eyes moved quickly over the brief text. Sweat gleamed on his narrow forehead despite the cool breeze blowing off the Canal.

"It refers to someone named Helen Creel and to the therapist whose photograph is on the front," Urbino said. "But you understand English. It also mentions the Barone. He's been threatened several times, and Barbara is worried that this is another threat," Urbino explained vaguely. "Do you know this therapist?"

"She works at the hotel."

A look of withdrawal came over Zeoli's lugubrious face.

"Do you know who Helen Creel is?"

"Is this a guessing game?" he snapped. "They sell those cards all over Abano! I have no idea what this is about."

Urbino could scent fear on Zeoli as unmistakable as the sulfur that emanated from his skin and clothes. Unless Urbino was completely misreading the man's response, he not only recognized Helen Creel's name but associated it with something far from pleasant.

Not to seem too eager before asking his next question, Urbino stared silently out at the palazzi lining the Grand Canal. On the right was the Guggenheim Museum, one of whose paintings had recently helped him reach some answers in a delicate investigation that had also involved the Contessa. Encouraged by this reminder of a past success, he looked across the Grand Canal to the Casetta Rossa. It was in this small red house that D'Annunzio had lived during the First World War and, blind in one eye and lying immobile, had written his memoirs.

But it was less these details that Urbino considered now than a pomegranate tree, planted by D'Annunzio, that flourished next to the building as a reminder that the past was never really dead.

"There's another thing," he said in what was perhaps too casual a voice, turning back to Zeoli. "It's about the murder of the couple in the Rialto Market. Did you notice anything about either of them at the reception that might be even remotely significant? Something you overheard, something you saw? Anything?"

Zeoli looked stunned.

"Nothing! And there's absolutely no relationship between them and the center—none whatsoever—if that's what you're suggesting!"

When the boat was pulling into the San Marco landing, Urbino brought up Harriet's visit to Zeoli the night of the murders.

"She stopped by to talk about treatments at the spa. You know how—how concerned she is about her health. I don't remember exactly what time she left. Excuse me."

Zeoli got up and pushed his way through the crowd in the cabin. By the time Urbino got off the boat, he was nowhere in sight.

That evening Urbino, with his cat Serena curled on his lap, tried to put the case in the back of his mind, where, he hoped, wonders might somehow be worked on it. He wanted to read nothing that would remind him of the murders or the Barone and opened a familiar volume of Henry James. It was a story, like most of James's, in which the deaths were natural and the only violences were the cutting words, turned backs, and whispered rumors of the drawing room. This was the kind of world he himself preferred, the one he had tried to create for himself here in Venice. Ironic, then, wasn't it, that he found himself involved in yet another murder investigation!

But perhaps not so strange, really. His serenity had once again been shattered, this time by Bobo and the murders in the Rialto. And he hadn't been in the best frame of mind to begin with, not with his recent gout attack that had so prostrated his body and his spirit. He had to get to the bottom of things and then his world would be in order again, wouldn't it?

Not quite, not if Bobo remained in the picture. If he did, things would never be the way they used to be, and this realization caused him a pang. If it hadn't been so late, but especially if Bobo hadn't been staying with the Contessa, Urbino would have called her, perhaps even gone to see her.

When he tried to escape into the pages of the James story, however, he found he had, after all, made a poor choice in his reading material. It was a sad tale of the drift of a man too proud and self-absorbed to recognize and return love until it was too late. Certainly a more disturbing tale for the midnight hour than any ghost story could be.

He snapped the book shut and got up, sending Serena springing to the floor. A few minutes later, his scarf wrapped tightly around his throat against the cold, damp night air, he was striding away from the Palazzo Uccello. The *calli* were almost completely deserted. It was a clear night and he could see the stars overhead. He briefly considered going to the Ca' da Capo but turned in the opposite direction.

He soon found himself standing on the Rialto Bridge, all its shops long since shuttered. He looked down the broad sweep of water lined with Gothic and Renaissance palazzi. The three-branched iron lampposts and a few random lights from the private residences and hotels were reflected murkily in the Grand Canal. At the moment no boat broke its still surface. He had a partial view into someone's apartment through a window. A bookcase, a portrait of a nude woman, a Murano chandelier.

He was now standing at what had once been the commercial heart of Venice. Banks, insurance companies, a stock market, artisans' workshops, stores, warehouses, a clandestine slave market—they had all made this area buzz with getting and spending, with business and barter. The top-heavy quality of the Rialto Bridge had always struck Urbino as appropriate, considering the burden of ducats that had been made and lost on its high arch and in the surrounding area. The Rialto was still very much of a bazaar, its shops crammed with jewelry, trinkets, and vegetables, but it was a mere shadow of its former grandeur and power.

This was the place and the hour Moss and Quimper had met their deaths. They too might have walked over the bridge and paused like this to look down at the untroubled scene, have peered into the same window, little knowing that in a matter of minutes they would both be brutally murdered a short distance away.

But perhaps they hadn't been blithe at all that foggy night, but filled with trepidation and some presentiment of what was about to happen. Surely they realized the danger they had put themselves in by threatening Bobo?

Urbino turned from the parapet and went down the bridge toward the green market. He walked beneath the shadows of the Church of San Cassiano, with its huge twenty-four-hour clock, then past the crouching stone figure of the hunchback of the Rialto. Had Moss and Quimper peered nervously beneath the arcades of the Fabricche Vecchie very much as he himself was now doing?

A few moments brought him to the Erberia on the Grand Canal. Wooden and cardboard crates, wooden price signs, and stray pieces of fruits and vegetables littered the darkly shadowed stones. There was a deathlike stillness.

He walked along the water's edge to the *traghetto* station from where passengers were ferried to the other side of the Grand Canal. It closed every night before nine so there was no chance that, even if the fog hadn't been a problem the night of the murders, one of the *traghetto* men might have seen something.

But this wasn't exactly where Moss and Quimper had been murdered, and he felt he needed to go there. He crossed the marketplace to the roofed area of wooden storerooms. Despite the hour the door was still open and Urbino thought he heard voices from somewhere among the warren of storerooms. He went in. The urinals were still illuminated so perhaps the attendant hadn't forgotten to lock up but was still there.

A church bell tolled the first hour of the new day. Hoping that he might be somehow inspired by the grim associations of his surroundings, he walked past the rows of slatted and wired-enclosed storerooms to the bank of the Grand Canal where it made a sharp curve by the massive stone arch of the Rialto Bridge. It took little imagination to add to the scene Moss's and Quimper's bloody, lifeless bodies sprawled on the stones, thick fog drifting around them.

But who else had been there? Who had lain in wait or stalked them? Bobo came too easily to mind. It couldn't have been him, even if he couldn't account for his time during the crucial period. No, Bobo couldn't have been the one—although perhaps he hadn't called Festa on the Flora telephone but Moss and Quimper to set up a deadly rendezvous. But if he hadn't called Festa, why had she lied? Perhaps she desperately needed to protect herself as well. She had been out with Peppino after Moss and Quimper had left the hotel. Maybe she and Bobo were acting in concert? They could even—

Urbino stopped himself from building his house of cards any higher. It was his dislike of Bobo that was enticing him on. He had to keep an open mind—yet surely not if it meant ruling out Bobo when he should be putting him as squarely within the picture as anyone else.

Pits and traps all around him. Urbino turned away from the Grand Canal. Being here, perhaps a little foolishly, at the exact hour of the murders had brought him little more than confused thoughts. Maybe tomorrow at Abano he would start to get the kind of answers he needed. With this hope, he walked back in the direction of the main door.

Urbino picked his way carefully through the area of storage rooms. He heard a sound behind him as if one of the wooden crates had been pushed a short distance against the stone pavement. He stopped and listened, but the sound didn't come again. Then suddenly a cat darted past him. Giving a silent little laugh of relief, Urbino continued toward the door. When he saw that the lights were now off in the urinals, he quickened his pace, fearing what he might find. Yes, the door was now locked tight as several pushes and nudges showed him.

"Is anyone there? I'm locked in."

His own voice echoed back at him. He waited a minute or two by the locked door. Maybe there was another way out. He searched among the storerooms but didn't find any, then went back to the Grand Canal. But he realized there was no way out here either. The other door was locked and the massive Palazzo dei Camerlenghi at the foot of the Rialto Bridge walled him in.

There was one passageway he hadn't yet tried. It was even more shadow filled than the others. He made his way carefully down it. At its end was a fence of wooden slats, several of which were missing, others broken off. The opening was narrow and about three feet from the ground. He found a crate, climbed on it, and put one leg through the opening. So far so good, but this was the easy part. He next stuck his head and upper body through and for several moments didn't quite know what to do, hanging as he was half in, half out. He must be a ridiculous sight—not to mention an easy victim. This latter thought got him pulling his other leg through the opening, but only to have the material of his pants get caught on a nail. The only thing he could do was pull and pull hard. Which he did, making a large tear in his pants but managing to free himself.

He dropped to the pavement and hurried over the Rialto Bridge, feeling not a little proud of himself for an escape which, although not exactly graceful, had been agile enough to show him that his future might not necessarily be one of gouty immobility.

Gemelli called Urbino the next morning. Marie Quimper's sister had arrived and wanted to talk with someone who had known her sister.

"Didn't learn much from her," Gemelli said. "But see what you can do. As for Casarotto-Re's clothes, no traces of blood at all were found on them. And his medical records show that he *is* susceptible to spontaneous nosebleeds."

Gemelli sounded irritated.

Urbino told him about the postcard from Abano, saying he would bring it to the Questura later today or tomorrow. He said nothing about his own plans to go there today. His silence puzzled him. What was behind it? He felt that his judgment was becoming more and more mired.

A few hours later, sitting across from Urbino in one of the frescoed public rooms of Hotel La Residenza, Anne Quimper seemed almost nunlike in her stillness. She was younger than her sister, with a smooth, pale face and short brown hair. She wore a simple black dress and kept her hands clasped loosely in her lap.

"The concierge told me that Vivaldi was baptized in the church," she said quietly, nodding down at the simple brick facade of the Church of San Giovanni in Bragora. "Marie loved Vivaldi. She was very talented," she said. "Not only in languages, but in music, painting. I looked up to her. The Commissaire tells me that you knew her."

"She was very much like yourself," Urbino said after he had described his contact with Marie Quimper. "Quiet and gentle."

"Oh, much better than I! It broke our family's heart when she moved to London two years ago to teach. She would come back to visit us several times a year—until she met that dreadful man. No one in our family ever met him. She sent us photographs. She was crazy about him. They met at the school in London where they both taught. He was an artist, but I never heard of him. Marie said he would be famous someday. I admit he was good-looking, but he wasn't good for her."

"What do you mean?"

"What do I mean? She's dead, isn't she? I saw her body!" Her voice had risen, but only slightly, and now she put her face in her small hands. She must have been crying, for her small shoulders heaved, but she did it silently. She took her tearstained face from her hands and said: "It's *his* fault, be sure of that! Whatever happened was because of him! He made her life miserable, but she was in love. In love!" she repeated scornfully.

"What do you mean Moss made her life miserable?"

"He was insanely jealous! He wouldn't let her out of his sight! The one and only trip she made home after she met him was a horror! He called day and night to see where she was. God forbid, if she was out! Marie thought it was romantic. Proof of love! But I saw it for what it really was. Sick! I wouldn't be surprised if he beat her, but of course she never would have told us that."

"When was the last time you heard from her?"

"She called on my birthday three weeks ago."

"Did she say anything about her plans, or about Hugh Moss—or about anything at all—that might give us some idea as to what happened to the two of them?"

She shook her head slowly.

"Nothing, but she always spoke well of him. She was afraid not to. I asked the Commissaire if he was sure that Hugh didn't shoot Marie and then himself. He said it was impossible. Oh, Monsieur Macintyre, I hope they find out what happened so that Marie will be avenged! The Commissaire didn't come right out and say it, but I could tell that he thinks Marie was doing something wrong. I told him that wasn't possible, that it was something Hugh was involved with." She touched his arm. "If there's any way that you can help, please do it! My sister was innocent of any wrongdoing!"

"You can help yourself, Mademoiselle Quimper. Tell me. Did your sister ever mention a place called Abano? It's a thermal spa north of here."

"Abano? The name is familiar. She was here in Venice before, of course, but I'm not sure about Abano."

"She was in Venice before?"

"About a year ago with Hugh—and to one or two other places in Italy, too. She sent postcards. Maybe I can find them at home if it's important."

Urbino remembered how Moss said that this was their first trip to Venice. He took out the postcard of Abano spa. When he handed it to Anne Quimper, her eyes widened. She turned it over and looked at the address.

"The Contessa da Capo-Zendrini? The Commissaire mentioned her name and the name of a barone. I never heard of either of them. But this is one of the cards I got from Marie that time!"

"Are you sure?"

"I remember it very well. I thought it was a strange postcard to send." She pointed to the photograph of the woman therapist holding a bucket of mud. "Marie said something about her. That she was upset because Hugh was spending a lot of time talking to her."

"Did she ever mention this woman again? Or a woman named Helen Creel?"

"Nothing, Monsieur."

"And the printing. Do you recognize it?"

"It's not Marie's. I never saw Hugh's." She thought for a second. "If Hugh sent it to this Contessa, might it have something to do with their murders?"

"That's what I intend to find out, Mademoiselle Quimper."

18

Urbino recognized the woman immediately. She was older now and her red hair had considerably faded, but she was definitely the same woman. Her name was Stella Rossi and she was on her break at the café across from Zeoli's thermal spa. A faint odor of sulfur surrounded her. Urbino introduced himself and the Contessa, who had insisted on accompanying him. When he showed her the postcard, she drew her breath in sharply.

"Please! Don't make any trouble for me."

"We have no intention of doing that, my dear," the Contessa said. "Do we, Urbino?"

She gave him an admonitory look.

"Or for the center," Stella Rossi added. "That would be just as bad. I've worked there for nineteen years. I don't want to have to leave. Signor Zeoli told me that a man would come asking me questions and that I must watch what I said. We've always had a good relationship. He'll be our next director."

Urbino and the Contessa hadn't seen Zeoli—had in fact made a point of avoiding his office and making their initial inquiries at the reception desk.

"I should tell you, Signora Rossi, that the Venice police will be coming here to talk with you and probably Signor Zeoli. You see, this involves murder."

"I know, Signor. Murder and suicide."

She said it wearily, as if it were an old and familiar tale. There it was again, wasn't it? The assumption that Moss had killed Quimper and then committed suicide. Zeoli must have told her that Urbino would ask about the couple. But surely something was wrong, for Rossi was now saying, "It's burned into my mind. I'll never forget it."

"You were there?" the Contessa asked.

"Of course I was! That's why you've come to speak with me, surely? So that I can tell you all about it."

She could see they were confused. She snatched up the postcard and turned it over, frowning down at the writing.

"It's addressed to you, Contessa. I don't understand English, but it mentions poor Helen."

The Contessa's puzzled expression deepened.

"As well as you and a man called the Barone Casarotto-Re," Urbino said.

Rossi shook her head.

"I've never heard of him."

"You see, Urbino, this whole thing is absolutely ridiculous. Bobo—"

Urbino gave the Contessa a look and she fell silent. He now realized what Rossi was referring to. Oriana had brought the topic up at the Contessa's reception in front of Moss and Quimper.

"When you just mentioned a murder and suicide," Urbino said, "you were referring to the murder of the woman in one of the therapy rooms, weren't you?"

"Of course! That's what you want to know about, isn't it?"

"Urbino, whatever are you talking about? The murder of a woman here? I thought you wanted to ask her about Moss and Quimper."

"I'll explain later. Please tell us about it, Signora Rossi. Tell us about Helen Creel."

After ordering another coffee, the woman began.

"It was an August afternoon twelve years ago, right before Ferragosto. Signor Zeoli arranged Helen Creel to be my last appointment because I had to get to Rimini for my holiday. She was beautiful and spoke good Italian. I had given her two other treatments. She hurt her elbow playing tennis, but I think she came for a rest. Many of our patients don't come only for the treatments. They come to get away from the world outside—their jobs, their families. We have strict orders to protect their

privacy about schedules, treatments, even whether they're staying at the spa at all.

"Helen Creel was English but her husband was an American
colonel from the base near Vicenza. They had a son about
twelve or thirteen. He came to the spa with Helen, just the two
of them. Very quiet, a nice-looking boy. Helen was crazy about
him but not about her husband. Patients sometimes talk a lot,
especially with me. Helen was a real talker. She told me her
husband was insanely jealous, always suspicious, following her
around, asking her to account for every minute of her time. I
don't know if she gave him any reason to be like that. I never
saw any evidence of it but some men don't trust the best of
women, believe me.

"She was going on the same way on that August afternoon. I
had just finished applying the mud." She nodded down at the
postcard, on which her younger, smiling self held a bucket of
mud. "Helen seemed nervous. She kept looking at the door."

Rossi was becoming more disturbed. She shook her head
slowly, a strangely blank look in her eyes.

"Suddenly the door burst opened. A man stood there, looking
at her. Helen started to sit up. Then everything happened so fast.
The man raised his hand and there was an explosion. Helen fell
back on the bed. There was another explosion and her head
twisted. She was looking straight at me and there was blood—and
bone—and—and other stuff. Oh, it was terrible! My face was all
spattered. There was another explosion and after that one, Helen
just—just sank back on the bed and sighed. Her husband—
that's who it was, of course—stood there for a few more seconds,
looking at her coldly. Then he ran down the corridor. He went up
to her room and shot himself right in front of their son."

The Contessa had become increasingly aghast during Stella
Rossi's account and now she said accusingly to Urbino in English: "What a horrid tale you've subjected us to! Even to suggest
that it might have something to do with Bobo is pure insanity
and—and a betrayal of every trust I've ever placed in you!"

Urbino ignored the Contessa's outburst and asked Rossi in as unemphatic a voice as he could muster if she had ever seen Signor Creel before he came to the therapy room.

"Never," she said with an apprehensive glance at the Contessa. "He wasn't staying at the hotel. I don't know how he knew how to find Helen."

Urbino reached into his jacket pocket and took out the photograph of Bobo that Harriet had given him the night of the Contessa's reception—the photograph he had shown to the guard at the Doges' Palace. The Contessa paled.

"Signora Rossi, have you ever seen this man before?"

She looked down at the photograph and nodded her head.

"Yes. He's very handsome. I haven't really *met* him but I've seen his photograph before."

"In the newspaper?" the Contessa asked, breaking her short silence with what was almost a shout.

"Oh no. A young Englishman showed it to me. Not the same photograph, but it was him. More than a year ago. He came here with his girlfriend. French, she was."

Urbino and the Contessa exchanged a quick glance.

"I never saw either of them before. They weren't here for any treatments. Just for the day. The man showed me the photograph and asked if I knew who it was. I told him no. He was disappointed, but his girlfriend seemed happy, as if I had said what she hoped I would. He didn't tell me who the man was or why he was interested in him."

"Did either of them mention the murder of Helen Creel?"

"No."

Urbino thought for a few moments, then said: "Has anyone else been here recently who was interested in the story of Helen Creel?"

"Yes, Signor, two weeks ago. An Italian gentleman here for treatments. An asthmatic. We have a new therapy for asthmatics—exercise and mud on the chest and back. It does wonders." She seemed about to become sidetracked into a professional

126

testimonial, but pulled herself back: "He asked me what I knew about Helen Creel. I never heard of her, I said. He was very persistent, but what could he do when I kept denying it? I warned my colleagues. He asked some of them questions but they didn't tell him anything. After all, it's *my* story," she said with a sudden, perverse burst of proprietorship and pride. "I hope that nothing I've said is going to make any problems for me or the center?"

"Not at all, Signora Rossi," Urbino assured her. "Just be sure to tell the Venice police what you've told us. You've been a great help."

The look on the Contessa's face, however, showed that she was nowhere close to agreeing with him.

A far from companionable silence dominated their return to Venice. The Contessa hoped the silence, mainly of her own making, would be more uncomfortable for Urbino than it actually was, but he was too lost in thought to feel it keenly. He was going over what they had learned from Stella Rossi, and what it meant to the murders of Moss and Quimper.

Only when the *motoscafo* was pulling into the Ca' da Capo-Zendrini landing did the Contessa break the silence.

"This has nothing to do with Bobo. It's an elaborate web you were supposed to unweave, *not* get caught in!" She added, not able to resist in her passion gilding the lily, "And *not* add your own strands to, thank you very much!"

The Contessa refused Urbino's help and alighted from the boat. She made further, almost comical demonstrations of independence as she bustled ahead without a glance back at Urbino, who felt like a disgraced footman.

He was several paces behind her and had a good view of the

firm set to her shoulders and the upward tilt of her head. He
caught up with her at the door of the *salotto blu* where she
stood looking at the scene within. Bobo was on one knee in
front of Festa, her face strewn with tears. He held one of Festa's
plump hands in his and was rubbing it. Peppino was yapping at
his ankles as if he were assaulting his mistress. Festa was the
first to recover from what seemed to be the shock of the Contessa's arrival. At any rate, she spoke—or rather shouted—first.

"Orlando is dead! Just like Rosa—and on the same day!"

Bobo relinquished Festa's hand and stood up, managing,
with a deft but firm maneuver, to kick aside the still-yapping
Peppino. He brushed off his pants.

"The same day?" He seemed genuinely puzzled and disturbed. "Is it really, Livia?"

The Contessa, finally deigning to turn her head in Urbino's
direction, said: "*Now* see what's happened!"

Then she swept into the room with the air of leaving Urbino
to contemplate his own culpability.

"There he was! Lying in the bed, his eyes wide open! Grasping a page of crumpled newspaper. It was terrible!"

"How did you come to find him?" asked the Contessa, drop-
ping onto the sofa next to Festa.

"I have a key to his room. He insisted the desk give me one
after he collapsed at your reception. I looked in on him every
morning."

"What time did you find him?" Urbino asked.

"Really, Urbino!" the Contessa said with a touch of exasper-
ation. "Must you be so persistently *yourself*? Give us all a
chance to adjust to this new blow."

"I—I didn't know anything about that," Festa said. "So you see, when he didn't answer, I became very concerned. Poor Orlando. He might have fallen or had an attack, I thought. I went right to his room and let myself in with the key. I called his name but he didn't answer. I found him just as I've described and went down to the desk." She contemplated her clasped hands. "It was such a shock to me. You can imagine."

"Especially since he seemed fine last night about ten," Bobo said, "but these attacks can come on suddenly."

Urbino noted the precision with which both of them gave the time.

"He had his inhaler," he said, remembering it within easy reach next to the photographs of Gava's dead relatives. "Did you see it, Livia?"

"It must have been there somewhere."

The Contessa's mouth was set in annoyance as she glared at Urbino. Nonetheless, he risked another question.

"Exactly when did Rosa die, Bobo?"

"Rosa has nothing to do with *any* of this."

Bobo's face was closed, as if guarding a secret.

PART THREE

Desire and Pursuit

1

The next morning at the Questura, after Urbino told Gemelli what he had learned at Abano, Gemelli said: "And now the man who seems to have been nosing around there is dead."

Gava had died of complete respiratory failure sometime between midnight and six in the morning. His inhaler was found in the garden beneath his open window. Only his fingerprints, and those of the hotel employee who found the inhaler, were on it.

"Gava could have made those threats against Casarotto-Re and planted the evidence in the couple's room," Gemelli said.

"But Gava didn't kill them! If anything, he was killed because he knew who the murderer is or maybe he was killed to lead us down the wrong path."

"Perhaps." Gemelli lit a cigarette and inhaled deeply. "Something has surfaced. Your Contessa withdrew a large sum from the Banca Commerciale Italiana the other day."

A chill fell over Urbino.

"Don't forget that she's assuming almost all expenses for the bridge of boats."

"It was a *cash* withdrawal."

"What you're implying is that the Contessa has turned over this money to the Barone."

"We'll just wait to see if the money turns up in the *right* hands. But you could find out more quickly. You're her friend."

"The Contessa is far more likely to accept an intrusion by the police than by a close friend!"

"True enough, but you're in a better position for damage control. And however closely attached she is to Casarotto-Re, she'll cut the strings immediately if she believes she's being used for his own shady ends."

"You don't know the Contessa at all," Urbino said, wondering how much he himself could claim to know her these days. "She's a faithful friend."

"A 'faithful friend,' yes, but what about a 'woman scorned,' even a 'lover betrayed'?"

The Commissario's smile leered at Urbino through a thick cloud of cigarette smoke.

"Livia Festa said that she has a key to Gava's suite," Urbino said, hoping to move things away from the Contessa. "But he didn't seem to like her and didn't want her poking around in his affairs."

"*Had* a key. We have it now. She says Gava got an extra one from the hotel but no one supports her story. We're making the rounds of the likely places it could have been copied. Festa claims she didn't touch anything in the room. Clear thinking under the circumstances. But why aren't her fingerprints on the doorknob? Because she wore gloves! At eight-thirty in the morning to step down the hall? A maid saw her come out of Gava's door. White as a sheet, she said, and carrying a large pocketbook. She didn't say anything to the maid about Gava being dead. The maid went to make up the room next to Gava's. Doesn't know if Festa returned to her own room or not. We never would have heard about that key if the maid hadn't seen her. The maid knows her work schedule precisely. Says Festa came out of Gava's room about twenty minutes after eight. She didn't show up at the desk until eight-forty. Claims she came directly down. I doubt it."

So did Urbino. Festa had made too much a point of saying she had found Gava's body at exactly eight-thirty.

"You think Festa murdered Gava?"

"Possible, but maybe she was just checking to see if the deed had been done. Tidying up, so to speak."

Scattering ashes over the pile of papers on his desk, Gemelli fished out one sheet and handed it to Urbino.

"A list of Gava's possessions."

Urbino ran through the items. Near the top were the photographs Gava had called his "portable graveyard." Gava had said they would probably be thrown away once he died, a day that he had said wasn't too far away. A premonition? Or could he have had reason to fear for his life?

"The lab is running tests on the medications. One bottle was completely empty. Thrown into the wastebasket in the bathroom. The bottle had the name of a drug that retards attacks."

Urbino continued to stare at the list, puzzled but not knowing exactly why.

"It seems he had only one inhaler."

"Found in the garden two hours before Festa discovered his body."

"But why throw it out the window?"

"To make it look as if Gava died because he didn't have access to it after it had 'accidentally' fallen, I suppose."

"He seems to have died on the same day his sister did—and in the same way. He was depressed about the anniversary of her death coming up, maybe even afraid. And another thing. Moss knew who Gava's sister was. And now Gava is dead as well as Moss and Quimper."

"*Cherchez la femme!* Or *les femmes*: Gava's sister, Helen Creel, and Festa! And what man is in the middle of them all? Casarotto-Re, who's now bestowing his favors on your Contessa! Maybe she'd be interested to know that a waiter at Harry's says Casarotto-Re and Festa were holding hands the night Moss and Quimper were murdered."

"They considered marrying once. Maybe that explains their closeness."

"Depends on how you look at it. The waiter also says they were arguing furiously at points. About what he doesn't know."

2

On his walk from the Questura, Urbino suddenly realized how nervous he felt—nervous about what Gava's death meant.

It wasn't just that he now had to reconsider the direction he had been moving in, perhaps retrace his steps to some crucial earlier point to prevent himself from becoming completely—disastrously—lost.

Gava's death, following so closely after Moss's and Quimper's murders, couldn't be a mere coincidence. It had to be related to the bloody scene at the Rialto. Surely he couldn't now be faced with two different murderers.

Gava had died little more than thirty-six hours after their conversation at the Flora. Had this conversation led directly to his death? Had he passed something on to Urbino that someone wanted to be kept a secret?

Urbino remembered only too well his feeling of panic when he had found himself locked in the area where Moss and Quimper had been shot to death. Had this been an accident? Or had someone deliberately locked him in, to stalk him, to do him serious harm? This had happened only a few hours before Gava's death. Perhaps someone had wanted to get rid of him and Gava both as soon as possible. If this was the case, then surely the murderer was watching for another opportunity to get at him.

If it were only himself he had to be concerned about, it would be bad enough, but there was the Contessa. She could be in danger, and much of it could be his own doing. He was going to have to proceed more carefully.

He sat down on a bench in a quiet square. Laundry flapped in a chill wind. Dark clouds were reflected in large pools of water. A little boy ran away from his mother and splashed through a puddle, calling out, "Kwah, kwah, *acqua!*"

He focused on the list of Gava's possessions. Maybe one of the items would provide a clue. He wished he had copied them down and tried to remember them as best he could. The framed photographs, a box of loose photographs, medications, the empty bottle found in the bathroom, the inhaler, the previous day's newspaper grasped in his hands—

Suddenly he realized what had been puzzling him at the Questura about the list. He went into a café on the square and called Gemelli.

"An address book? I don't think so. Let me check." After a few moments in which the only sounds were the striking of a match and the rustling of paper Gemelli said: "There isn't any. Are you sure?"

"Positive. I had to take it off my chair before I sat down. It was leather covered, about six by four inches."

"So someone took it, before or after Gava's death."

At that moment Livia Festa and the Barone Bobo were in the *salotto blu* of the Ca' da Capo-Zendrini. The Contessa was at the municipal offices on business involving the bridge of boats.

"Damn it!" Bobo said. "It's taking forever!"

Bobo and Festa looked at the fireplace where the flames were consuming a small book with a leather cover. Peppino was asleep on the settle.

"Couldn't you have just taken the page?"

"Ripped it out and left the rest? How long do you think it would take the police to figure it out?"

"You might have taken two or three pages. That would have set them back."

"I'm sorry that I don't have your presence of mind! Remember that Orlando was staring at me! But I was very careful. I wiped everything, even the doorknob."

"Fool! Your prints *would* have been on the doorknob!"

"I didn't know I'd see the maid, though, did I? And I couldn't just go back and put my prints back on! You're being unreasonable. Besides, I told the Commissario that I was wearing gloves."

"Just as bad! Gloves to make a visit of charity first thing in the morning!"

Together they watched the flames start to burn the leather cover. When it was finally unrecognizable they both breathed more easily.

"Now for this," Festa said, holding up a sheet of paper on which there were several handwritten lines followed by a signature. It didn't take long to burn. "And this." Festa added two typewritten sheets. They curled, blackened, and disappeared except for wisps of ash. The little book had been consumed.

"A regular bonfire," Bobo joked.

"Let's hope I found everything. If not—"

Bobo kissed Festa's plump, rouged cheek.

"Think positively, *cara*. That's the way I'm getting through this. It's going to be all right. You'll see. We'll have smooth sailing before too long."

"Before too long! Years! I don't see why you can't be content with what I'll have—what *we'll* have—from Orlando."

"A drop in the bucket, *cara*, to what the Contessa has lying around the palazzo."

Festa stood up angrily.

"That bitch thinks she can buy whatever she wants. She thinks she can buy *you!*"

"No one buys me! Ever! And don't forget it!"

Once again they lapsed into silence. They were sitting like this, with the appearance of two longtime friends for whom conversation wasn't always a necessity, when the Contessa came in.

"Livia! What a delightful surprise!" The Contessa's eyes

darted around the room and seemed to pause when they took in the fireplace. "It *is* a bit chilly out." Walking closer to the fireplace, she cast a quick glance into the fire. The face she turned to the couple didn't reveal whether she had noticed anything unusual among the flames.

As Urbino approached the main door of the Ca' da Capo-Zendrini, Festa hurried out. She was frowning furiously and carrying Peppino with less ceremony than usual. The dog's expression matched her own.

"Livia! I'd like to talk with you for a few minutes."

"Not now if you don't mind," she said curtly, not even breaking her stride.

Inside the palazzo Urbino found the Contessa about to go down to the *motoscafo* where Bobo was waiting with Milo. The Contessa looked radiant. She was wearing a new floral-print dress and, if he wasn't mistaken, a new scent.

"I'm sorry, Urbino. Bobo and I are on our way out. But I have something to tell you." She lowered her voice. "I heard from Laura today." Laura was her contact in the Milan fashion world. "She told me what she already knew and was able to find out about Flint. He appeared on the scene ten years ago. He had a good career going for about five years but then things started to fall apart. There was talk of drugs and big debts and some unsavory connections. He was on the fringes of Cinecittà for a while. Then he set himself up as an art consultant. He always seemed to be out of money, but he always had well-off friends, usually women. But I don't think either of us should say a word to Oriana, not yet. She won't thank us for it and—and well, people *do* change."

This facile observation ended their conversation and Urbino went down with her to the boat landing. As Bobo was helping her into the boat, she lost her footing slightly.

"Careful, my dear! You've become a little careless lately. It's a blessing you haven't had a serious fall!"

After the Contessa and Bobo had left, Urbino went up to the *salotto blu* to fix himself a drink. As soon as he entered the room, he caught the sharp odor of smoke. He went over to the fireplace and bent down to look into the fireplace where ashes smoldered.

Hesitant footsteps entered the room. They paused and came toward the fireplace. Urbino stood up. Harriet jumped like a frightened cat and dropped several magazines. Urbino picked them up. They were health and fashion magazines as well as some brochures of the health spas at Abano Terme.

"Oh, it's you, Urbino!"

"I'm sorry, Harriet. I didn't mean to startle you."

"Is—is Barbara here?"

Her eyes strayed in the direction of the fireplace.

"She just left with Bobo." Urbino handed her the magazines and brochures. She seemed eager to leave. "Just a moment, if you don't mind, Harriet. I'd like to ask you some questions."

Fear raced over the woman's plain features.

"Does the name Helen Creel mean anything to you?"

"Helen Creel?"

"She was mentioned on the postcard you handed Barbara the other day. An English woman murdered at Marco's spa twelve years ago."

"Marco Zeoli and I are only acquaintances. He doesn't gossip about his spa, and if he did, I wouldn't be interested!"

"You've had occasion to visit him rather late in the evening."

"If you must know, it was about treatments."

This was what Zeoli had told him.

"Actually, I'm more interested in your walk back from Marco's that night. I was wondering if you might have seen something which, however farfetched, might throw some light on what happened? It doesn't take anywhere near an hour and a half to get back here from San Polo. Maybe you were sitting at a café or looking down at the Grand Canal from the Rialto Bridge as I often do late at night."

"If I had noticed anything at all, I would have informed the police long before this. I never went anywhere near the Rialto Bridge. I crossed the Grand Canal by the bridge at the railway station. As I told you and Barbara that night, I got lost in the fog. Now, if you'll excuse me, I have work to do."

Outside, Urbino glanced at the lowering sky. A chill wind was blowing in from the lagoon. Wherever the Contessa and Bobo had gone, they would return before long. The Contessa hated being on the water in a storm. Violent weather could blow up very quickly at this time of the year. It was the season of the *acqua alta*, the treacherous high water that threatened the city and had done so much damage in '66. He hoped that there would be good weather for the Contessa's procession to the cemetery island, which was only three days away.

At the bar, he ordered the Campari soda he hadn't had in the *salotto blu* and went over what the Contessa had learned about Flint. Not much of it surprised him, least of all the man's need for money and his association with well-to-do women. Could Flint have been somehow involved in the threats against Bobo, have seen it as a source of financial gain? He had had more contact with Moss and Quimper than anyone. He and Oriana had met them at the Grassi exhibit, introduced them to Urbino at Harry's Bar, and accompanied them to Bobo's opening night. He had even gone with Oriana to the Flora the morning after the couple had been murdered to see if they wanted to join them on their jaunt to Chioggia. And Flint lived not far from the Rialto green market. Urbino had to find out what he had been doing on the night of the murders, but first he had to talk to Marco Zeoli again.

By late afternoon, when the weather had finally turned to storm, the Contessa and Bobo hadn't returned. As his water taxi made its choppy way on the Grand Canal, Urbino peered through the window to see if he could catch a glimpse of the Contessa's boat. All he could see was a rain-lashed, impressionistic blur, and he soon gave up.

The water taxi left him on a *fondamenta* near the Zeoli apartment. As he was dashing through the rain past a trattoria, he saw Zeoli sitting inside, his only company a liter of red wine. Urbino went in. He took off his dripping coat and wiped his face with a handkerchief.

"May I sit down?"

He didn't wait for an answer but slipped into the seat across from Zeoli.

Zeoli, his elongated Goya face more somber than usual, got another glass and poured some wine. The aromas from the kitchen made a nauseating mixture with his sulfurous odor.

"You've come here about Helen Creel," he said in his cold, exact voice.

"Stella Rossi told you."

Zeoli nodded. There was a greater air of weariness and sickliness to him today. He obviously needed a rest far away from sulfur, mud, and restorative waters.

"But I saw you and the Contessa. It didn't take much to figure out why you were there. I suppose you want me to corroborate her story."

"Yes, but I could have done that in other ways. What I want to know is why you didn't tell me yourself."

"You must be joking! I didn't want the Creel story dredged up. It's long since forgotten."

"Obviously not. Don't forget the postcard. And Rossi said that a couple—apparently Moss and Quimper—were asking about the Barone a month ago. They showed her his photograph. Did they speak with you?"

"No."

Zeoli poured the remaining wine into his glass.

"What about Orlando Gava? Did he ever ask you about the Creels?"

"No."

The mention of Gava's name had brought no discernible reaction. Urbino studied Zeoli's face as he asked: "Do you know that he's dead?"

It hadn't been in the paper yet.

"Dead?"

He seemed genuinely surprised.

"Livia Festa found him in his suite at the Flora. It seems he died of pulmonary failure sometime between midnight and six yesterday."

Relief flooded Zeoli's long face.

"That means that three people associated with the Creels are dead," Urbino said.

Zeoli smiled without any humor.

"Is that a warning to me? Good thing I was with my mother in the apartment from ten on last night or else I might have been set upon in a dark *calle* by this roving, mad murderer you have in mind who kills by shooting and causing pulmonary failure. As for Helen Creel, I hardly knew her. It happened right after I came to the spa. She was staying with her young son. Her husband—an officer in the American Air Force—shot her in Rossi's therapy room. Then he went up to her room and shot himself in front of the son. That's it."

"One thing puzzles me. Rossi claims no one gave Colonel

Creel any information, yet he knew exactly what therapy room to find her in—and what room she and their son were in."

"Helen Creel probably told him herself."

"Rather unlikely. Rossi says she wanted to get away from her husband."

Urbino and Zeoli sat silently, looking out at the rain.

"I'd like to know about the Creel son," Urbino eventually said.

"He was just a kid, thirteen, fourteen. I've often thought how terrible it was for him to have his father shoot himself like that right in front of him."

"Scarred for life, you can be sure. He'd be in his mid-twenties now." Urbino paused. "I assume you didn't recognize him. Stella Rossi didn't seem to either."

"What do you mean?"

Zeoli's hand holding the wineglass shook slightly as he waited for Urbino's answer.

"I believe Hugh Moss was Helen Creel's son."

Urbino walked to the boat landing in the rain. Some areas were flooded and the planking hadn't been put up yet, so he had to retrace his steps. He regretted not having brought an umbrella until he saw all the twisted remnants littering his route, victims of the wind that whistled through the narrow alleys with diabolical malevolence.

Once in the boat that rocked on the heaving waters of the Grand Canal, he considered what he had learned from Kolb and Zeoli. Both were nervous and both were lying: Zeoli about the murder of Helen Creel, Harriet about her walk back from Zeoli's the night of the murders.

One of the hardest problems in his investigations was sorting out the lies. There were always so many, but very few had to do with the crime. Most were benign or self-protective or sadly habitual. Before he could identify the deadly ones that concealed villainy of the darkest kind, he had to consider—and discard—all the others, which were often the murder's greatest camouflage.

What might he be missing? What wrong assumptions could he be making? Was his dislike of Bobo leading him into one error of judgment after another? Had it exposed Gava to danger and eventual death?

Urbino tortured himself with these questions as the boat made its way up the Grand Canal through the heavy rain.

As a biographer he was accustomed to search a person's life for the meaning behind its outward show, to delve into his past for the essential clues. He often thought of this past as a bridge, sometimes light and airy, more often ponderous, occasionally dark and funereal, that had to be crossed, one difficult step at a time, before he had any chance of understanding his subject.

If the taunt behind the Abano postcard wasn't just a devilish prank, Moss's and Bobo's pasts had the same somber shadow, the murder of Helen Creel. What other links—call them steps on the bridge—did the two men have in common? Or was this one enough to have led to the violence on the Rialto?

By the time he reached the Palazzo Uccello, soaked to the skin, his mind was a hornet's nest of different versions of how, given what he already knew and suspected, Moss and Quimper had met their bloody deaths.

And no matter what version it was, Bobo was always standing there ominously in his field of vision.

If the Contessa had been in a different frame of mind, she might have found it unusual that two rooms just happened to be available at the Locanda Cipriani on Torcello. But she was too preoccupied with the storm to reflect on what powers of persuasion or planning Bobo, whose storm eye had been honed by years of idling along the Mediterranean coast, might have used.

"We can't possibly go back tonight, Barbara," Bobo said over dessert in the Cipriani dining room. Outside, the storm howled furiously.

Unbidden, to the Contessa's mind came Ruskin's words: "Mother and daughter—you behold them, both in their widowhood—Torcello and Venice." She shivered and took a sip of her coffee.

"Everything's been taken care of. Milo found a room in one of the farmhouses. Consider it fate," he said, covering his hand with her own.

"So this is where Hemingway wrote that dreadful book about Venice," the Contessa said later, up in her room. "All bird shooting and drinking at Harry's."

" 'Dreadful'? The good old colonel who 'kisses true.' "

She gave him a tentative smile.

"You look lovely tonight. If I'd known how fear makes you blossom, I'd have seen to it that you got a pleasant little fright from time to time."

He laughed and put his arm around her shoulders.

"You've been abstracted all day, Barbara dear. Since last night in fact. It's Orlando, isn't it? But there's nothing to be done there."

"To die all alone like that, and just like Rosa," she said, echoing Festa's words yesterday. "But it's not just Orlando."

"What is it, then? You're not ill, are you?"

"Not ill, no. But I do have a headache."

Bobo kissed her forehead, then poured himself some champagne. He sipped it with a reflective look. "It doesn't have to do with your trip with Urbino yesterday, does it, *cara*? Where did you go?"

"Abano."

As soon as she said it, the Contessa felt a peculiar and paradoxical sense of release and fear. She looked at Bobo. His face was mildly curious. She realized where she was heading but she couldn't hold herself back.

"Oh, Bobo! We had the most frightful time. We heard a story that I just can't get out of my mind."

She rubbed her forehead as if she were indeed trying to erase the memory of Stella Rossi's account. After pouring himself more champagne, Bobo pulled a chair next to her and took her hand.

"Perhaps if you tell me, *cara*, you'll feel better."

With Urbino's warning not to tell anyone sounding only faintly in her ears, the Contessa began.

Urbino called the Ca' da Capo-Zendrini at ten o'clock that night and learned that the Contessa and Bobo still hadn't returned.

He chose a book, this time one less unsettling than the James of the other night. He got into bed, Serena snuggling by his side, and gazed down at the book without reading it. Instead he began to ponder the case.

Given what he had learned, if the murders were an elaborate, diabolical attempt to frame Bobo, the murderer was not only someone emotionally disturbed, and hiding it well, but also someone intimately familiar with Bobo's past. Perhaps this person even now had—or had had before—an intimate relationship with him.

But Bobo as a victim on this scale? Yet all Urbino had to call to mind were Bobo's haughtiness, his egotism, his insolence, his deceptiveness—oh, Urbino could go on and on!—and it was plausible. Bobo was the kind of man to incite hate and resentment as well as, apparently, love.

Urbino next considered possible motives other than this one of intense, personal hatred for Bobo. There was financial gain, since Moss's and Quimper's knowledge could have tempted someone to turn this knowledge into gold. And the Contessa had recently made a large cash withdrawal from her bank. Urbino had little doubt that she had given this money to Bobo and that he had turned it over to someone else.

Another motive was self-protection. Although Moss and Quimper—and Gava, if he, too, had been murdered—had probably endangered no one's life but their own, they very well could have threatened something even less bearable for a certain kind of person: loss of reputation.

And then there was a motive of twisted benevolence: to protect not the murderer but Bobo or someone else the murderer cared about very deeply.

Urbino started to try to line up the likely candidates in each of these disturbing categories, but eventually, despite an exercise as unlike sheep counting as an exercise could be, he drifted off into a haunted sleep.

The Contessa was drowning in the lagoon as Urbino struggled to reach her. An excruciating pain in his foot, monstrously swollen, made almost all his efforts futile. She kept moving farther beyond his reach, flailing, crying out for help. Suddenly Bobo emerged from beneath the waves like Neptune, his handsome head cascading water. He ignored the Contessa's desperate pleas and swam forcefully, purposefully, toward

Urbino, who let himself drift down to the bottom of the lagoon.

There, amid the mud and weeds, lay a crystal coffin. Reclining inside was Harriet Kolb, whose short brown hair had turned gray and was now voluptuously long. In her hands was a burst pomegranate, its fatal, crimson seeds staining the front of her white dress. As she turned her head and began to scream, Urbino woke up. He was sweating and his heart was racing.

Three-fifteen. He wanted to call the Ca' da Capo, but restrained himself. Instead he took two sleeping pills and read until he drifted off into a dreamless sleep.

He was awakened by the phone at eight-thirty the next morning. As he reached for the receiver, he could tell by the quality of the light through the shutters that the storm had cleared the weather.

"Barbara!" he said.

"Sorry to disappoint you. It's Gemelli. Thought I'd give you the latest developments. Gava's will. A copy was found in that box of loose photographs. We somehow hadn't noticed it before. Made out nine years ago. We're trying to locate his lawyer in Rome. Guess who benefits?"

"The Barone?"

"Not a lira! The bulk goes to the medical school in Bologna in memory of his sister. There are small bequests to his sister's nurse and some servants." When Gemelli paused, Urbino knew the important part was coming. "And then there's Signora Livia Festa: she comes in for triple my annual salary. 'To Livia Festa, for her love and regard for my sister.' She said she knew nothing about it."

"Livia Festa!" Urbino was now fully awake.

"Maybe Gava was trying to say something to Casarotto-Re by giving the money to Livia and not him."

Or something *about* him, Urbino said to himself.

"Item number two," Gemelli said. "We got a phone call from London. Moss's uncle. He's flying in tomorrow with his lawyer. It seems this isn't the first time someone in his family has been murdered in Italy. His sister, twelve years ago. And you'll never guess who she was."

"Helen Creel, Hugh Moss's mother."

"You already knew, Macintyre? I thought we were supposed to be cooperating!"

"Why wasn't Hugh Moss's last name Creel?"

"His uncle raised him after Creel murdered Moss's sister and killed himself. Had his name legally changed."

"Does he know who the Barone is?"

"Never heard of him. Said there was absolutely no reason for Creel to be jealous, but you know brothers. It doesn't take too much to figure out that Casarotto-Re was having an affair with the Creel woman and that her husband found out. And the son inherited his father's jealous streak. Exactly how all this led to what happened in the Rialto green market is the big question. Casarotto-Re has even more to explain now. There's something else. Casarotto-Re had an argument with Moss a short time after leaving Festa at the Flora. In Campo San Luca." Campo San Luca was not far from the Rialto Bridge. "Two men resembling Casarotto-Re and Moss exchanged blows in the presence of a woman. By the way, we've been trying to contact Casarotto-Re since last night. Neither he nor the Contessa has returned our calls."

Knowing what Gemelli's reaction was bound to be, Urbino said quickly: "They went out together yesterday afternoon in the Contessa's boat and weren't back by ten."

"And they probably aren't back yet! Why the hell didn't you call us? Who knows what's happened to them—or to *her*, is more like it! We're going to start looking for them right away."

After Gemelli hung up. Urbino called the Ca' da Capo. The Contessa and Bobo weren't back yet.

An hour later at the Flora he learned that Festa was walking Peppino in the Giardini Reali. Before he went in search of her, he spoke with the maid who had seen Festa coming out of Gava's room.

"Gloves, Signor?" she said. "She definitely wasn't wearing gloves. I saw her rings flashing as bright as fire."

In the Giardini Reali Peppino pulled at his leash, his mouth covered by a fashionable leather muzzle. Festa, dressed in her characteristic robe and turban, chided him affectionately as she explained to Urbino that she had never laid eyes on Flint before Bobo's opening night.

"Not at Cinecittà and not in Milan. And I don't recall seeing him in *Uomo Vogue* or any other fashion magazine either, although I suppose I must have if he was as successful as you say. But good-looking men are a dime a dozen in my world. For me to notice them—to remember them—they need something more than a pretty face."

"He hung around Cinecittà," Urbino persisted.

"Has he said he knows me?"

"No, I—"

"There you are then."

They walked under the cast-iron arcade, avoiding the puddles that reflected a blue, cloudless sky. Mothers with youngsters were chatting with each other on the benches. A woman, dressed in a Missoni sweater and carrying a Bottega Veneta bag, was distributing fresh fish to a passel of cats. Beyond the gates of the gardens and the quayside kiosks selling souvenirs, the lagoon sparkled.

When they reached a little fountain, Festa said: "Let me tell you something about Flint. If I knew Oriana better I might say something to her. When we women are in love, we make fools of ourselves. Barbara—"

But she interrupted herself and quickly went on: "The other

day I was in a water taxi. When we were going down a back
canal near the Rialto, I saw Flint in a deserted *calle*. With another man—swarthy, beefy-faced, a perfect typecast for a
thug. Flint was showing the man a bracelet. Thank God, he
didn't see me. Maybe you should ask Oriana if she's missing
a diamond bracelet. It looked like a Bulgari I've seen her
wear."

Telling Urbino this story had given Festa evident satisfaction. A smile spread across her broad face. Could she be trying
to even a score? Urbino was reminded of her account of Moss
and Quimper in the Florence glove shop. What had Gava said
about her? That she prided herself on knowing things about
people? Sometimes knowledge of a certain kind could be dangerous for the knower.

Festa's story about the bracelet and the swarthy man rang
true. The Contessa's friend had mentioned Flint's need for
money and his association with an unsavory crowd. Then there
was his strange reaction to the phone call in his apartment.

Urbino felt, however, that Festa was trying to divert his attention. Did she suspect what else was on his mind?

When they sat down on a bench, he said: "You know about
Orlando Gava's will, don't you?"

"Since talking with the police I do. I had no idea. Orlando
was reticent when it came to things like that."

"His will mentioned your kindness to Rosa."

"I did what I could. The three of us took holidays together."

"In Taormina?"

"There—and other places."

Festa bent down to take off Peppino's muzzle. When she
straightened up, her large dark eyes were cold and ungenerous.

"Last week," Urbino said, "you implied that Rosa wasn't the
ideal her brother thought she was."

"Oh, she was a good enough sister!"

"But not a good enough wife, you mean."

Festa didn't speak for a few moments, but when she did the

words rushed out: "Rosa used her illness as a way of controlling Bobo, of arranging her whole world to her own convenience. You name it: furniture, meals, friends, the temperature in the house, everything! He had to walk on eggs, had to consult her about the simplest decision. It came close to ruining his art. Bobo is a good actor, and a good writer when the subject is D'Annunzio, but he would have been so much better without Rosa!"

"But she's been dead for ten years. Surely since then Bobo—"

"But can't you see? He was already formed! He was already ruined!" These were drastic words which she soon revised: "He had lost his drive. She had worn him down."

Bobo was one of the least "worn down" and the most aggressive men Urbino knew, but Festa might be right. His bravado could conceal a great many wounds, but how many of them could be laid at the door of Rosa, who had been considered a saint by her brother?

"Why didn't they divorce?"

Divorce had been legal in Italy for over twenty years.

"He had many things to take into consideration," Festa said with quiet emphasis.

"Like whatever Rosa would leave him in her will?"

"Is money such an unimportant consideration for you, Signor Macintyre? You seem to enjoy your creature comforts— the ones that you can provide for yourself as well as those your generous friends can." She let this hang in the air for a few moments. Then: "Bobo gave Rosa what she wanted. Was it unreasonable for him to expect her to—to make it all up to him in the end?"

"I assume she did?"

"The Gavas had a lot of money."

Some of which was soon to go into her own pocket.

Festa put the muzzle back on Peppino and stood up.

"I have to be going," she said.

Urbino said nothing until they reached the gates.

"Did you notice an empty medicine bottle in the wastebasket in Orlando's bathroom?"

"I don't look through people's trash!"

"Unusual that the bottle was thrown away, isn't it? He would have saved it to be refilled."

Festa shrugged.

"Orlando was a strange man." She seemed about to let this stand, then added: "We're all going to miss him."

She arranged her round features into a good semblance of sorrow.

"Just one more thing. About discovering his body. You told the police you were wearing gloves." They both looked down involuntarily at her ring-studded fingers. "And in fact your fingerprints weren't found on the doorknob. But the maid insists that you weren't wearing gloves that morning."

Festa stopped, bringing Peppino up short on his leash.

"She doesn't know what she's talking about! You don't have to pass any intelligence tests to become a maid, not even at the Flora! Good day!"

After she stooped down to pick up Peppino and walked indignantly over the bridge near Harry's Bar, Urbino called Gemelli from a nearby phone box.

"Look into the death of Rosa Gava Casarotto-Re in Taormina ten years ago. Probably the same day that Orlando Gava died," Urbino reminded him.

"John's at home, Urbino dear," Oriana said over the phone. "Neither of us saw anything that night, thank God! We were here—the whole night. Filippo had business down in Rimini. And no, I'm afraid I don't know where Barbara has disappeared to, but don't worry. She can look after herself. They probably found some cozy hotel somewhere. Barbara's in mad, marvelous love! Let her be! This doesn't happen that often in a person's life, especially someone Barbara's age. As for my own sweetheart, I'll call him to tell him to stay put until you get there."

Half an hour later Urbino was looking up at Flint's building from the other side of the little square. He was about to cross the square when the door of the building opened. A swarthy man with a briefcase came out and gave Urbino a quick, appraising glance before plunging into the *calle* that twisted its way toward the Rialto Bridge. Urbino waited a few moments before ringing Flint's bell.

"What do you want now! Haven't you got—" Flint shouted in surprisingly colloquial Italian and without the trace of a drawl. He broke off when he saw it was Urbino. "Urbino!"

"Could I talk with you a few minutes?"

"I was just going out. Let me get my jacket."

Flint locked the door. When they were in the square, Flint guided Urbino in the direction opposite to the one the swarthy man had taken. Flint ran on about the storm last night, his Southern accent getting thicker and thicker. He and Oriana had watched most of it from the living room of the Ca' Borelli. "Reminded me of the storms you and I have in our part of the country," he said, apparently aiming for a note of national fellowship. "God, the way they come sweeping in from the Gulf! I remember one when I was nine or twelve years old. Half the county was flooded and—"

Flint exuberantly continued his reminiscence. He was more at ease the farther they got from his apartment. From the storm he went on to enthuse about something he had come across in an antique shop in the Dorsoduro quarter.

Urbino patiently listened to his description of an ebonized vase stand by Brustolon similar to the ones at the Palazzo Rezzonico. He made appropriate comments and noted the former model's nervous energy. It was only when they emerged from the damp and dark of the alleys into the bright air and light of Campo San Polo that he was able to broach one of his reasons for seeking out Flint.

"I'm trying to piece things together about the night Moss and Quimper were murdered. It's important to gather every scrap of information, no matter how insignificant it seems."

"I'm sure that's true."

"For example, they went from the Flora to the Rialto. Some-one must have seen them." Urbino saw no reason to divulge their encounter with Bobo in Campo San Luca. "Perhaps you've forgotten, or perhaps someone has mentioned seeing them to you."

"And who would have done that? I was with Oriana the whole evening—and night," he emphasized. "It's not as if Ori-ana and I are suspects, is it? Ha, ha!"

His laughter echoed across Campo San Polo.

"Don't forget what happened to the Baron Corvo," he said.

Flint smiled but his eyes didn't look amused.

"He lived in that palazzo right across the way, didn't he?" Flint continued. "His hosts gave him the old heave-ho when they saw how he had abused their hospitality in his book. Fi-delity to one's friends—and the friends of one's friends! Can you imagine Oriana's reaction if she knew we were on your list, however far from the top? By the way, if you turned your talents to Corvo, I'm sure you'd do a wonderful job. You should do a book on him."

"Perhaps I will one of these days. You were at Cinecittà after leaving modeling, I believe," Urbino said to get things back on track as they walked across the square toward a café.

"Only for a short time. It didn't suit me."

"Did your and Livia Festa's paths cross there?"

"I was introduced to her on a set. I doubt if she remembers, though."

He waited for Urbino to confirm this but Urbino knew the virtues of waiting.

Flint broke the silence when they reached the café and did it in a rapid flow: "You're asking about Festa because you think there's something strange about Gava's death, right? You probably think it has something to do with the murders. Oriana and I know Festa found the old man's body, but from what I could see she's never acted at all suspicious. You could be right, though. Whoever murdered Moss and Quimper must have done in old Gava. It makes perfect sense. Maybe I can move farther down your list when I tell you I was playing cards with my landlady and her brother in her apartment above mine until the wee hours of that morning."

"Thank you for the alibi, but I haven't said a word about Gava."

"You didn't have to! I can tell you think it's all connected. And I think so, too! Find Gava's murderer and you'll find Moss's and Quimper's."

"That could very well be," Urbino said. "In all your contacts with Moss—"

" 'All my contacts'!" Flint interrupted. "Listen to you! I didn't have very many!"

"More than anyone I'm aware of, with the possible exception of his murderer."

Urbino let this sink in for several moments as Flint stared at him steadily.

"Did Moss—or Quimper, for that matter—ever mention the name of Helen Creel?"

Flint wrinkled his brow.

"Helen Creel?" he repeated. "No, they never mentioned anyone with that name. I would remember."

Flint dropped into a café chair and motioned for the waiter. "Coffee? My treat."

Urbino declined and walked in the direction of the Rialto.

After leaving Flint, Urbino considered returning to Flint's building and asking his landlady about the card game. He decided against it, however. Even if he might be able to get her to answer his question—and getting people to do this when he had no official status with the police was often impossible—he didn't think it a good idea. She might tell Flint that he had been to see her, and Urbino didn't think this was a good idea.

Besides, Urbino somehow sensed that Flint would never have given himself the alibi of the card game unless it were true. His landlady, unlike Oriana, would not be so quick to lie for him.

What had Flint said? He had been playing cards until the "wee hours." Say that it was three, even four o'clock, when they had stopped. It still would have been possible for Flint to go to the San Marco area, slip into the Flora, and kill Gava.

Possible, but rather unlikely. Surely he would have been noticed going into the hotel at that hour. Venice started dying many, many hours before that.

Instead of continuing straight ahead to the Rialto, Urbino wandered through the twisting *calli* of San Polo, preoccupied with a hundred questions and his increasing nervousness over the Contessa's absence.

Wooden planks were still set up, but most of the water from the recent storm had either dried or subsided back beneath the paving stones. Within a few minutes he gave himself up completely to his thoughts. The external scene of crumbling palazzi and crooked bridges and deserted squares soon receded into the background.

Brooding made his steps random, his turnings unmindful,

and he eventually found himself in an unfamiliar, empty *calle*. Recognition would surely come at the next turning or from the name of the *calle* painted on the side of one of the buildings.

But when he reached the end of the narrow *calle* and looked down the next one he still had no sense of where he was. The name on the flaking building was not one he recognized. In rapid succession he felt humbled, irritated, and then tense, for he couldn't shake the sudden feeling that someone was following him. Whether this came from a sixth sense or was the residue of his anxious minutes locked in the Rialto green market, he didn't know, but it was very strong.

He went down the *calle*, listening for footsteps behind him. He heard none. But this didn't lessen his growing feeling of panic as images of the bloody bodies of Moss and Quimper flashed before his eyes. Pounding in his head was the thought he had had earlier, that the violence wasn't over yet.

When a familiar square opened ahead as if to mock him, Urbino was surprised to find how far he had wandered from his route. He tried to reassure himself that his frantic moments just now had been caused by nothing more than an overexcited imagination and continued in the direction of the Ca' da Capo-Zendrini.

In a few minutes he was standing on a bridge gazing at a crumbling palazzo. He often came here to look at this particular building for it was the one Henry James described in a story of deception surrounding the private papers of a famous American poet. The old palazzo had a garden, unseen from the bridge, which figured prominently in the story and which also had been visited by Napoleon. Urbino had once stood in the middle of the wildly overgrown garden, and still remembered the sense of melancholy and mystery he had felt.

But this afternoon the garden's associations were far less with Napoleon and James than with Bobo and the murders on the Rialto, for D'Annunzio had described the fruit-and-jasmine-scented garden in *Fire*, where he likened it to the "soul of the exile." Bobo had interwoven parts of the description into *Pome-granate*.

The evening of the Contessa's reception Moss and Quimper had been wandering through the much different garden of the Ca' da Capo. Had they had a rendezvous with someone? Had anyone overheard their conversation in the pergola? Urbino tried to remember where everyone had been at that time, which had been right before Gava's collapse.

Yes, it might help to know, as it would surely help to know exactly where Harriet and Bobo had been during the time of the murders. They both claimed they had been on walks, but perhaps their walks had taken the same path. Perhaps they had even been walking together.

Harriet seemed afraid of Bobo now, but perhaps the Contessa had been right. Perhaps Harriet had fallen in love with him. Once in love, she could have been used by him in some way and was now regretting it.

Urbino, considering these new possibilities, left the bridge and walked briskly toward the Ca' da Capo.

"Don't look at me like that!" the Contessa said later that afternoon when Urbino walked into the *salotto blu*.

"Like what?" he asked. He wasn't sure which of his several feelings he had conveyed. His surprise, his irritation, or, in fact, his admiration, for the Contessa looked particularly attractive as she sat on the sofa in a shaft of sunlight.

"As if you're looking at a ghost."

The image, given the way she seemed to glow with health and vitality, was so inappropriate that he smiled.

"Does that smirk mean that you're not upset with me?"

"I've been worried sick about you, and you know it! Where have you been?"

"Torcello."

"Torcello! Since yesterday afternoon?"

"You saw what that storm was like! Thank God, there were two rooms at the Locanda Cipriani."

"A real stroke of luck. You could have called me! The phones weren't out. But I suppose you didn't even think of it. There've been two murders—maybe three, counting Orlando." He fixed himself a drink and sat down. "And Bobo? How is *he* doing?"

"Not well at the moment. He took to his bed as soon as we got back. It may be the flu."

"I want to talk with him."

"You're going to have to wait! And so will Gemelli. He's left half a dozen messages. I won't have either of you pestering the poor man with your silly questions."

She watched him as he took a sip.

"It's obvious you're not in the mood to tell me what this is all about."

"Do you really know anything about my moods these days, Barbara?"

Fortunately, the Contessa was relieved from answering by the entrance of Harriet, her face pale and drawn. She handed the Contessa a folder.

"My God, Harriet! You look completely knackered!" the Contessa said.

This only made the secretary turn paler.

"Go right home, my dear. Even better, stay here where you can be looked after properly. We'll have the doctor in for you and Bobo both."

"Oh no! I'll be fine back at my place, really! I think you'll find all those letters in order. Excuse me."

When Harriet had gone, the Contessa said: "I suspect that might be an example of unrequited love."

"Do you still think she's pining away for Bobo?"

"Who else? Oh yes, I forgot! Marco Zeoli. Well, perhaps you're right, but the man had better see what he can do for her before she collapses completely."

"What do you know about Harriet, Barbara?"

"What do I know about her? She's the best secretary I've ever had!"

"And her references?"

"Impeccable! What *is* the matter with you this morning, Urbino? Now dragging in poor, defenseless Harriet!"

She went into one of her sulks which experience told him could last longer than his own patience. She usually could be jollied or coaxed out of them but this afternoon he didn't have the inclination. Well, she was already upset, he might as well go all the way.

"I have to ask you about something, Barbara. Gemelli knows that you withdrew a large sum from your account at the Banca Commerciale Italiana and that—"

"He *what*! How dare he! I'll have him sent straight back to Sicily, and don't think I can't, don't think I won't!" She glared at him. "How could you let him do such a thing!"

"I'm hardly in a position to prevent the police from doing what they want to do—and need to do. You have to be protected."

"Deliver me from such protection, Sir Galahad! I can take care of myself, thank you! What I do with my money is entirely my affair! Alvise never put any strictures on it. I've given generously, as you're very well aware! And I've given with some good sense, too, I hope, and I don't need you or Gemelli asking me to render an account like some shopkeeper on the Rialto!"

This reference to the Rialto, reminding her of the murders of Moss and Quimper, sobered her. She looked at Urbino with an almost desperate expression: "I'm in so deep, aren't I? I feel like I'm about to drown."

And she did indeed take a long, deep breath as if in search of the air she needed.

"Do you think I want to feel this way? Do you think that if I could *be* any other way, I wouldn't?"

When Urbino said nothing, she glared at him as if he had voiced his deepest criticism.

"I don't care what you think! I don't care what anyone thinks! The only person who really understands is Oriana."

"Oriana! Don't be a fool! I hope you're not using *her* as a role model! Oriana and her string of gigolos!"

"I'm well aware that Oriana isn't exactly a saint but she isn't afraid to feel! She follows her heart, wherever it leads."

"To her and Filippo's destruction one of these days! But you might get there before her! Excuse me, Barbara. I think it might be better if I leave. I'll stop by later when Bobo's had enough beauty sleep."

On the *traghetto* ferrying him across the Grand Canal to the San Polo quarter, Urbino stared straight ahead at the farther shore, ignoring the chatter of two old women behind him.

He didn't regret anything he had said to the Contessa. He had a responsibility to save her from herself. Yes, he was jealous, but it wasn't making him completely blind to what was going on—and it definitely wasn't putting ideas in his head! Bobo was not to be trusted. If he was nothing else, he was a liar and a deceiver, and this was danger enough for the Contessa.

And she seemed to be having second thoughts. What had she said? That she was in deep, that she felt she was drowning. Was it possible that she knew something about Bobo that she was keeping to herself, something that Urbino should know? Her defiant exclamation that she had to follow her heart could be a sign that she herself was beginning to fear where it was leading her.

The best way to protect the Contessa was not to dismiss his suspicions of Bobo as mere jealousy. He was convinced that the more he learned about Moss and Quimper and the night of their murders the closer he would come to Bobo's true villainy.

Urbino stepped off the gondola and made his way quickly to the Zeoli apartment. Marco shouldn't be back for at least another hour, and then he would have his winding-down time at the trattoria.

The nurse answered the bell and led him to a dark room. The only source of light was a flickering television, its volume turned up high. The nurse left.

Urbino was about to introduce himself when the wizened old woman sitting on the sofa shouted: "You're Signor Macintyre, the American! Marco talks about you. Maybe you want more light. Young people don't like the dark. Just pull the curtains back."

He went over to the window and pulled the curtains aside. Affixed to the outside of the window was a little mirror positioned so that it reflected a piece of the scene in the *campo* in front of the Zeoli building.

"It's enough of life for an old woman," Signora Zeoli said, noticing him looking at the mirror. "Along with *that*." She nodded her white head at the television where Zorro was riding away. "You can put the sound down."

"It's obvious that your son looks after you," Urbino said after adjusting the volume.

"You don't have to be so sly, young man! Trying to get on my good side like that. We've never met, not me and you, or me and that fancy Baronessa or Contessa or whatever she thinks she is." She stared at the television screen for a few moments, then relented enough to add: "She's kind enough to Marco. I guess that's supposed to be enough for me. But just because I can't go to her fancy balls or whatever they are is no reason for her not to come here!"

"I'll extend your invitation."

"Don't you do anything of the kind! I'll chase her right back to that museum of hers! Why don't you just ask me what you came to ask me, young man, and forget about being polite! It's a waste of time."

"I appreciate your honesty, Signora. I want to ask you about the murders in the Rialto green market last week."

"The young couple shot to death. You'd have to be dead yourself not to know about it."

"Have you heard anything from your friends in the quarter that might help the police find out what happened?"

"Nothing! And don't think my Marco knows any more, because he doesn't! He would have told me. Anyway, he was here in the apartment all that night. He's been in every single night for the past few weeks to keep me company—except for the Contessa's ball," she added quickly. "I hope you're as good to your mother."

"He had a visitor the night the couple was murdered."

"He certainly did! Scrawny woman, thin as a broom handle, with a pinched face. The secretary of this Contessa. Why a single, solitary person needs a secretary I'll never know. Well, she seems to have got one that can't even push a pencil or whatever they do these days. Always sick, to hear her talk. Maybe she thinks Marco has a cure for her."

This sent her into peals of laughter which precipitated a coughing fit. Urbino gave her a drink of water.

"What time did Signorina Kolb leave that night?"

"The same time Marco told you if you've asked him," she snapped. "Almost eleven."

Harriet hadn't returned to the Ca' da Capo-Zendrini until at least twelve-thirty.

"Much too late to my way of thinking. Nervous as a cat, she was. Too keyed up to think that maybe other people wanted to get to sleep."

With what he was sure the direct old woman considered an

excess of politeness, Urbino apologized for having taken up her time. He turned the volume back up on the television and left.

14

"Bobo still isn't feeling well," the Contessa said coolly the next morning when Urbino went to the Ca' da Capo-Zendrini.

"Did you call a doctor?"

"He refuses to see one. All he needs, he says, is a bit of rest."

She looked as if she could use more rest herself. Yesterday she had said that she felt about to drown, and today an imaginative eye as well as a concerned heart could make out the telltale signs of her distress. The slight breathlessness. Eyes opened wide as if in search of something substantial to grasp. Even a faint air of desperation.

"Rest or not, I have to talk with him. I'd appreciate it if you would see that he makes himself available—for *your* sake as well as his. The best way to protect him—to show that you care about him—is to urge him to tell me everything that might be even remotely significant. And it's the best way for him to show *you* the same thing! I assure you, Barbara, he's hiding something and you're entitled to know!"

The Contessa stared at the Veronese over the fireplace.

"You confuse and frighten me these days!" she said. "Your behavior lately and all these terrible things have put my head in a whirl! I wanted to be in a completely different frame of mind for the procession to San Michele tomorrow night. However did it come on us so fast, I ask you? The Day of the Dead." She shook her head slowly. "There's always someone else to put on the dark list, isn't there? Now poor Orlando. Yes, Urbino, I'll speak to Bobo. I'll tell him to search every single corner of his brain to see if he can come up with anything that might help him. Us." She clarified: "The three of us. But you're wrong about him, believe me. You'll live to eat your words!"

She gave him a bright, brave smile.

"Tell me, Barbara, would Oriana be inclined to lie for Flint's sake?"

"I think, my dear, that a woman in love is likely to do worse things than that!"

"Oriana might well be in love this time, but Flint is shrewd. He's out for himself. By the way, I haven't noticed Oriana wearing her diamond-and-sapphire bracelet lately."

"The Bulgari? The one she got from Filippo's mother? You know, I don't think she *has* worn it recently. She loves it so— But what are you suggesting? Oh, I see! Flint has run off with it, is that it? Maybe you think Oriana should nail down everything in the Ca' Borelli. Maybe you think *I* should do the same thing! Fortune hunters hiding behind every gondola in Venice!"

There were so many things Urbino wanted to tell her, speculations he wanted to share with her, but a wariness now crept into his behavior with her. She might pass things on too readily and trustingly to Bobo, with possibly dangerous results. No, he would rather be there to see the man's reaction and to be the one to choose what Bobo knew and didn't know.

Mauro announced Livia Festa, who was right behind him, Peppino tucked under one arm. The two of them—dog and mistress—swept the room with eyes practically the same shade of dark brown.

"Is Bobo here?"

"I'm afraid he's indisposed," the Contessa said frostily. "Why don't you sit down, Livia dear. Would you like a saucer? For your dog, I mean."

" 'Peppino,' " Festa corrected. "No thank you on either count, Barbara. It's Bobo I've come to see. Forgive me for seeming rude, but I *must* see Bobo."

Festa's buxom body was tense. Hair was slipping from her snood and her makeup seemed to have been applied in a rush.

"But I've just told you, Livia. Bobo is indisposed."

"I've seen him more indisposed than whatever he's like now. More indisposed than you've ever seen him, I'm sure. I *must* see him."

"I'm afraid I can't allow it, Livia. This is my house. I have a responsibility to my guests."

"'Guests'! I like that! Don't you think you should find out if Bobo wants to see me? I think you'll find that he does. But don't bother. I'll go right up."

The Contessa and Urbino watched as Livia turned around and left, Peppino grasped tightly under her arm.

"Don't just gape like a fool! Do something!"

"What?"

"You're impossible! I'll show you what!"

He followed her out of the room, prepared to act as referee. But the Contessa had time to do nothing more than put a detaining hand on Festa's plump shoulder when Bobo emerged hesitantly along the corridor, wearing a dark purple dressing gown lined with gold silk and gold morocco slippers. He did in fact look ill. His face was more gaunt and his eyes had dark shadows beneath them. The smile he gave the two women and Urbino was a ghost of its former self.

"I couldn't bear lying in bed another moment. Even your beautiful Sargent was getting on my nerves, Barbara. That must show you what a state I was in."

The mighty organ of his voice was considerably diminished and as he walked toward them his step had little of its usual vitality.

"Get right back upstairs," the Contessa said. "Mauro! Would you come here and help the Barone back to his room?"

"Really, Barbara, that's quite unnecessary. If I could just sit down somewhere. And perhaps a cup of tea?"

"Mauro, help him into the *salotto*, please. Then tell Lucia to bring some camomile tea."

"Please, not camomile, Barbara! Darjeeling would be fine, and I don't need Mauro's help."

"I must talk with you," Livia said, putting her hand on his arm.

"Far be it from me to interfere," the Contessa said in a voice pitched above its normal register.

Bobo, now looking perplexed and a bit worried, said: "If I knew I was going to get this kind of attention, I would have come down earlier. What's going on?"

"I'm sure Livia will give you a full explanation. Urbino and I will be in the morning room. He'd like to speak with you when you finish with Livia, if you feel up to it. I think it would be a good idea for the two of you to have an open, honest chat. And, Livia, would you see that your dog doesn't sit on the furniture?"

Once in the morning room the Contessa sat down at the fin-de-siècle Viennese piano and started to play the movement of a Mozart sonata. The Contessa, who had been a student at the Venice Conservatory before she married the Conte, was a gifted pianist, but these days played only infrequently for others. Urbino sat back and listened.

The Contessa, all liquid fingers and rapt expression, was the mistress of an order and harmony that reigned all too briefly in the room. When she finished, the room seemed darker, heavier. The Contessa got up and sat beside Urbino on the sofa.

"Was that the equivalent of fiddling away while Rome burns, *caro*?"

"It was beautiful, Barbara. If life could be like that!"

"Like that on a good day, and a Jane Austen novel on a bad! But we unfortunately live in the nasty world, with uncivil souls like Livia. But I refuse to be discouraged by her kind! What I'm going to do, this time without the help of Mozart, is to try to comfort us with some much-needed clarity. I'll run through our list of suspects and give you the dubious benefit of my opinion."

She took a deep breath and began:

"Whoever murdered Moss and Quimper knew them and also knows Bobo." This immediately made it clear that she of course excluded Bobo from the list. "This wasn't a random act of violence, right? We have to ask ourselves what did the murderer gain by Moss's and Quimper's deaths. Motivation is the key. It's the sticky point, isn't it? Anyone could have obtained a gun in some way. As for opportunity during the crucial time, let's begin with Harriet," she said, showing less regard for her secretary than she had yesterday when she had berated Urbino for "dragging her in." "She was wandering around Venice after leaving Marco's. And what about Marco? What did he do after she left?"

Urbino told her that Signora Zeoli did in fact swear that her son had stayed in after Harriet left.

"There you are then! Let's next take a look at our dear and ever so gracious Livia! She left the Flora to walk that little beast about eleven, right on the heels of Moss and Quimper, but no one saw her come back! She could have tucked him right under her chubby arm and brought him all over town without any trouble. She's a determined little thing. Look at the way she just barged in here and imposed herself on poor Bobo! And," she added, obviously warming to the topic of Livia's suspicious behavior, "there's her connection to Orlando. She had easy access to his room with a key he might or might not have given her, and she was the one who found his body."

She frowned after saying this, perhaps realizing that by pointing the finger at Livia, she was pointing it a bit too close to Bobo. Urbino couldn't agree more.

"But what am I saying! I'm sure Orlando died a natural death."

"He could have died 'naturally,' but as a result of interference," Urbino allowed himself to suggest. "Someone could have emptied his medicine into the toilet and thrown his inhaler out of the window when he was having his attack—or before."

"I suppose so, diabolical and sadistic though it is," the Contessa said, clearly reluctant to pursue this line of thought either. "Let me see. Who else do we have?"

"There's Flint, although Oriana says they were together all that night," Urbino said.

"But what possible motive could he have?"

"You haven't really mentioned a motive for any of your suspects, my dear," Urbino pointed out, thinking of his own ruminations on the topic the other night. "Or means, either, although these days a gun could find its way into anyone's hands. But before we get to motive, let's clear away opportunity, and not just for Moss's and Quimper's murders but for Orlando's death, too."

"Orlando's?"

"Yes, to cover all possibilities. First of all, there are only two people with an alibi for the time of Moss's and Quimper's murders. One is Zeoli, as I've just told you. The other is Flint. Oriana swears they spent that night together at the Ca' Borelli. Filippo was down in Rimini."

The Contessa showed neither surprise nor disapproval.

"But as you yourself said about Oriana," Urbino pointed out, "a woman is liable to do worse things for someone she loves than lie." He paused fractionally, then went on: "As for Bobo, Festa, and Harriet, they have no one to corroborate exactly where they were between midnight and half past. And don't forget that Harriet was all out of breath when she came in that night and that Bobo had blood on his scarf, which might or might not have been his own."

The Contessa stared at him stonily for a few moments and said: "It's been my experience—or rather my observation—that murderers always have an alibi. The innocent see no need to."

"True, but having one is no more a proof of guilt than not

having one is a proof of innocence." Realizing that, after intending only to throw an oar in, he was now taking over, rather self-indulgently perhaps, all the rowing himself, he sat back and said: "But go on, Barbara."

"No, you go on. I don't feel up to it anymore. But if I don't agree, you can be sure I'll let you know."

She gave him a weak smile.

He gathered his thoughts and resumed after a few moments: "Staying with alibis and turning to the time of Orlando's death, we get this picture. Once again only Flint and Zeoli have alibis—which makes them doubly guilty by your rule of thumb. Zeoli and his mother both say he was at home again."

"We know how unimpeachable the word of a mother is!"

"Exactly. As for Flint, he claims he was in a card game with his landlady and her brother until what he calls the 'wee hours' of the morning. Although I haven't verified it, I think I have him figured out enough to know that he never would have said that unless it's true—and that he probably took away a large share of the winnings. I can't imagine him playing for any other reason, unless it was to establish an alibi. Of course, even if the game got over as late as four, which I doubt, he could easily have made his way over to the Flora in the given time and done what he wanted to do."

"Very improbable," the Contessa said with a trace of regret in her voice. "He could never have gone in and out at that hour without being seen."

"That's how I look at it. Harriet would have been noticed, too."

"Anyone would have. But even if that weren't the case, you can forget about Bobo slipping into the Flora through some back door."

"You can give him an alibi?"

The Contessa made a moue of distaste.

"I hope I don't have to 'give' him anything of the sort!" she said as if they were talking about something vaguely disrep- ·

utable or embarrassingly contagious. "But, yes, Bobo was with me!"

Urbino couldn't help but be reminded of what he had just said about Oriana, lies, and a woman in love. Surely the blush now spreading across the Contessa's face was, at least in part, caused by the same association of ideas.

"Are you saying that you definitely know that there was no time from midnight to six when Bobo could have left here without your knowing about it?"

The Contessa didn't answer right away. When she did, it was somewhat falteringly: "We—we weren't together the whole time, but I remember I didn't sleep well that night, and I would have heard him leave his room. He didn't." She added in a stronger voice: "He didn't, I tell you!"

"I'm sure you believe that, Barbara, and I hope it's true."

She seemed about to challenge this latter point but instead assumed a look of sufferance.

"At any rate, no one but registered guests were seen anywhere near the elevators or the stairway of the Flora," Urbino went on. "Which puts Livia in a bad light since she was already in the hotel that night—with a key to Orlando's room. And she was supposedly walking her dog when Moss and Quimper were murdered. But you know, Barbara, the fact that no one knows exactly when she came in creates a question in my mind. Perhaps we're wrong and someone might have been able to slip into the hotel unnoticed on the night Gava died."

"I don't think we're wrong, but suppose we're dealing with two murderers?"

"Very unlikely."

"Or suppose Orlando wasn't murdered at all?"

"Yes, a great deal hangs on the answer to that. Until we know for sure, we have no choice, as far as I see it, but to assume he was and that it was because he knew something that would lead us directly to the murderer's identity."

"Let's forget about Orlando. It will help us more if we stick to motives for the murders of Moss and Quimper since we have no doubt that they *were* murdered!"

"Well, if Flint's involved, it's got to be because of money. He never seems to have enough and he always has it on his mind."

He quickly told her what Flint had said at the Palazzo Uccello about her "generosity" and reminded her of what they knew about his days as a model. Then he described the incidents of the Bulgari bracelet and the man with the briefcase whom he had seen leaving Flint's apartment.

"But Moss and Quimper had nothing."

"No money, no, but they might have had something that could have been turned into money."

"About that murdered woman Helen Creel, you mean? But I don't see what Flint or—or anyone else has to do with that."

Urbino wondered if he was making a mistake—perhaps putting the Contessa in more danger—by not telling her that Moss had been Helen Creel's son and that Bobo had probably been her lover. But he held himself back now, tempted though he was, since there was some doubt about a liaison between Bobo and Helen Creel. He would wait until his talk with Bobo.

"I've remembered something, though," the Contessa said. "A rumor was going around this summer when you were out of town that Flint had forged one of Filippo's checks. Oriana swore on her mother's grave that it wasn't true, but where there's smoke there's fire. I promised her I wouldn't encourage the rumor but now— But how ridiculous! Oriana intimate with a murderer! It could never be. Love isn't that blind. Marco, then!" she quickly went on. "He was at Abano when Helen Creel was murdered. But what motive could he have?"

Urbino, who thought the Contessa's silence meant that she was pondering Zeoli's possible motive, was about to offer his opinion when she burst out with: "Harriet! Now, isn't she the one best placed to do some damage! She knows my affairs—my business," she corrected herself, "and don't forget that she handled some of the publicity for Bobo and that the postcard of

Abano passed through her hands. But I don't know! I can't see any motive for Harriet any more than Zeoli. Or for Livia either!" she added with almost a touch of pique.

Urbino thought very much the opposite about Livia. He told her about Orlando's will.

"Nothing for Bobo? But—but that's impossible! Whatever was he thinking of? And a generous sum for Livia! Well, there you are then! Just find some link between Orlando, Moss, and Quimper that involves Livia. Then you'll have it all in a neat package!"

Urbino silently disagreed, but only with how neat the package would be. It would be very messy, indeed, and it would almost inevitably involve Bobo.

"How well do you know Livia?"

"I know that I don't like her, and never have!" Then the Contessa relented: "But it doesn't make her a murderer—a triple murderer or a double murderer or any kind! I met her twenty years ago at the Venice Film Festival. She was just a scriptwriter then, although she had worked with some of the best. She was never a beauty and even then she was"—she searched for the right word—"*zoftig*, but she had a certain presence and determination that got her what she wanted—and *who* she wanted," she added after a pause. "She started to make films two or three years later. One of her films—all about sex, love, and death in Sardinia, you might remember it—got a lot of attention, but after that she seems to have lost whatever she had. Talent, patronage, drive? She went into debt and dropped from the scene for a few years, then began directing little theatrical productions. She puts up a good front, lives beyond her means. I wouldn't be surprised if Bobo helped her out from time to time, not that *he* has all that much, but they're old friends."

The Contessa paused.

"He was at the festival, too, alone," she said quietly after a few moments. "Rosa was ill. I always thought Livia was throwing herself at him, rather shamelessly really. Divorce had just become legal. Maybe she hoped he would divorce Rosa and marry her. But of course he'd never have done that and—and I'm sure it was all one-sided on her part. I mean, he didn't marry her *after* Rosa died, did he?" she added with obvious satisfaction. "Over the years, our paths have crossed from time to time. This is the longest exposure I've had to her and I hope it's the last! You just saw her behavior! How and why Bobo puts up with it is beyond me! Some men are better than they should be."

Was it Urbino's fancy that she seemed to say this with less conviction than she would have a short time ago?

Urbino told her what Livia had said about Rosa.

"She's wrong! Rosa was a sweet woman. Was it her fault that she was ill? Livia will never forgive Rosa for not having died sooner—or, more to the point, for not having left all her money to Bobo when she did. She probably figured she could get her hands on it some way."

"What do you mean about Rosa's money?"

"I thought you knew! She left everything to Orlando except for an amount to Bobo that's been enough to live frugally on, along with what he has himself. I can see your wheels turning! But Bobo *wanted* Rosa to do it. He said it was the only way he could show her that he really loved her." She shook her head with less conviction than irritation. "And now see what Orlando's done! Shut poor Bobo out completely! And left a tidy sum to that scheming woman! For her kindness to Rosa! Now, isn't that a laugh!"

The Contessa, however, was quite without humor.

Bobo, still in his purple dressing gown, sat on the sofa of the *salotto blu*, looking as if he were about to hold court. A

Gauloise dangled from one finger. Clouds of smoke hung over his head and drifted around the room.

"Ah! You don't even want any tea," he said to Urbino with a little smile. "That must mean you want to get right down to it. It appears that Commissario Gemelli is also eager to talk with me."

"Do you know why?

"No, but you're about to tell me."

Bobo leaned back, smoking his cigarette contentedly.

"You lied about the night of the murders. You were seen arguing with Moss in Campo San Luca an hour before they were murdered. What was the argument about?"

"As you just said, it was an *hour* before they were murdered and in any case Campo San Luca isn't the Erberia."

"But it's close enough. So you don't deny having an encounter with Moss and Quimper? It was Moss you called on the house phone at the Flora, wasn't it? Not Livia. To set up a meeting."

Bobo nodded.

"Why was Livia so quick to lie for you? Did she know about your meeting with them that night?"

"No!"

"Did she also not know about Orlando's will? Or that he disliked her—even though she says he gave her a key to his room?"

"It's not my business to answer for Livia."

"What was she so worked up about just now?"

"A purely professional matter about the show." He smoked his cigarette reflectively for a few moments, then said: "Underneath all of this"—he gestured at himself—"is someone with the full range of feelings. Sometimes I pretend otherwise. Sometimes I admit I get confused myself. But Barbara brings out the best in me. She lets me be me, the real me. Do you understand?"

"What does this have to do with your encounter with Moss?"

"Everything! Moss insulted her. Surely you and the police already know that from whomever it was who saw us in the Campo San Luca." Urbino gave no indication whether the substance of the argument had been overheard. "He said she was no better than Oriana, that she thought she could buy anything she wanted. He went on and on. An ugly little scene."

"But a little later he calls Barbara to tell her he's coming over. It doesn't add up."

Bobo snuffed out his cigarette in a Murano ashtray, a new accoutrement in the room since his arrival. He looked at Urbino for a few moments, then opened his arms wide and let them fall in a rather theatrical gesture of defeat.

"You're right. It doesn't 'add up,' to use your amusing little phrase. You see, Moss threatened to go to Barbara and tell her certain things. About something in my past."

"About Abano."

"If you're trying to impress me with your intelligence, you fail. It was only a small step from that postcard to finding out what happened to Helen Creel."

"Helen Creel, who was Moss's mother."

Bobo flashed a resentful look at Urbino, but when he spoke his voice was smooth and controlled.

"Bravo! That *is* quite a bit better. At any rate, when I saw that postcard I hoped Barbara would be spared."

"What you mean is that *you* wanted to be spared her knowing about Helen Creel, about your affair with her."

"Is that so strange? She's a sensitive soul. Murder and suicide are ugly, especially the Creel version of them."

"And of course you didn't want her to know that your relationship with Helen Creel precipitated the tragedy. She already knows what happened to that poor woman, but she doesn't know that you were involved."

"I'd prefer to tell her myself if you don't mind."

"I don't mind at all. In fact, I want you to do it as soon as possible. If you don't, I will, but I think enough of Barbara to realize that she would want to hear it from you. You should have told her long before this. When Moss threatened to tell her. If not then, then certainly after our trip to Abano."

The temptation for the Contessa to tell him what they had learned at Abano from Stella Rossi must have been great while she and Bobo were riding out the storm on Torcello. If she had, his not having told her immediately afterward about Helen Creel was strange, for what had he hoped to gain, since he must have known she would eventually know the truth?

The answer to his own question came immediately as Urbino sat there in front of Bobo: Time, the most precious of commodities.

"Tell me about Helen Creel."

"There isn't much to tell," Bobo said without any hesitation. "I met her in Milan twelve years ago. At one of the spring showings of a friend of Livia's. Helen and I took to each other immediately. It was a *coup de foudre* on both our parts. Helen didn't tell me at first that she was married and when she did, well, by then I had strong feelings for her. After about nine months we came to a mutual agreement. We would end our relationship." A troubled look passed over his face. "We said good-bye at the end of July. I went to Lago di Garda and Helen went back to her husband. They lived outside of Vicenza. The next I heard was that her husband had shot her to death at Abano and then killed himself. He was a very jealous man. His son inherited the trait."

"I suppose you'll say that was why you suggested to Gemelli that Moss might have killed Quimper and then himself."

"I don't like your implication! That's exactly what I did think."

"How did Colonel Creel find out about you and his wife?"

"I don't know. We were discreet. Even Livia didn't know about us. She still doesn't."

"Are you sure? More people might know than you think." When Bobo made no response to this intentionally cryptic comment, Urbino said: "Getting back to the night of the murders, you didn't return here for at least an hour after your argument with Moss. Weren't you afraid he was going to tell Barbara right after he left you?"

"I needed to clear my head. He led me to believe I still had time to decide what I should do."

"But by the morning he—and Quimper—were dead."

"I realize it doesn't look good for me. Now can you understand why I didn't want to say anything about my meeting with them that night—or anything about them at all? And how could I disturb Barbara? A woman like her shouldn't be tarred with even the smallest hair of a brush like that."

He looked at Urbino earnestly.

"I want to be completely frank, Urbino. No secrets. There's something else you don't know. It's an example of how Moss tried to keep me off balance. The day the threats appeared in the *bocca di leone* at the Doges' Palace I got a note signed 'Helen Creel' telling me to wait in the Sala della Bussola. I waited and waited and no one ever showed up. The guard was suspicious. Of course, I didn't want anyone to know I had been there once the threats were found. I'm telling you so that you'll have all the pieces."

"So you paid off the guard to keep him quiet after I first spoke to him."

Bobo shrugged in an affectation of helplessness.

"Guilty as charged, but I didn't lift a finger against Moss and Quimper to keep *them* quiet." Almost all his white, regular teeth flashed a quick, nervous smile at Urbino. "You must believe me, Urbino. They went over the Rialto Bridge to the San Polo side and I went for my walk."

The San Polo side of the Rialto was where the Erberia was—as well as the area where Flint and Zeoli lived, and where Harriet had been wandering after leaving Zeoli's apartment the night of the murders.

"Did you know that Moss was Helen Creel's son when you first met him here in Venice?"

"I only saw him once before, and he was just a boy then. No, he told me at the signing. He mentioned even then that he would tell Barbara. And he admitted that he had sent the threats. To let me know that I had been found out, is how he put it. He said that at that very moment one was somewhere in the bookstore."

"How did he know you were in Venice?"

"I can only assume he was keeping his eye on me through the press. Not very difficult. The show has been well publicized," Bobo added with more than a touch of pride. "There has even been some advance publicity in England."

"Has it occurred to you that someone could have told him exactly where you could be found?"

"Orlando?"

"He's one likely candidate. You probably thought the threats came from him at first, didn't you?"

Bobo nodded.

"He believed you neglected his sister, maybe he even held you responsible for her death in some way. You were involved with Helen Creel when you were still married to Rosa. And he was asking questions about Helen Creel at Abano."

"He was?"

Although Bobo gave a good imitation of surprise, Urbino sensed that he already knew—but from the Contessa or from someone else? Or in some other way? And if it hadn't been from the Contessa after her and Urbino's visit to Abano, had Bobo learned before Gava's death or after? These were yet more of the crucial questions swirling around the deceptive man the Contessa continued to trust.

"Perhaps someone else believed the threats were coming from Orlando, even though he wasn't at the signing when the last one was planted," Urbino continued. "Or maybe someone even knew that Orlando was aware of the Creel affair. This person could have killed him to keep him quiet—after having murdered Moss and Quimper. All to protect you."

"That's preposterous!"

"Or someone could be framing you."

Or Bobo himself could be going to great lengths to create one of these impressions, and doing a very good job of it.

"Take your choice, Bobo: a peculiar kind of friend or a diabolical enemy."

Bobo's face was set in a grim expression.

"More likely an enemy than a friend, considering something you don't know yet," he said and paused dramatically. "I received a threat *after* the murders, you see. On plain paper in a plain envelope with just my name on it. It didn't pass through the post but was slipped under the door here. The day before Orlando died."

"Slipped under the door? Which door?"

The Ca' da Capo-Zendrini had two doors on the land side. The first gave onto a small formal garden after which one reached the main door of the palazzo. Both were always kept locked.

"The main door, I assume. Harriet gave it to me. No point in asking to see it, though. I flushed it down the toilet. Not the right thing to do, but I wasn't thinking clearly. It wasn't just a threat. It was a blackmail note. A classic of its kind," he said dryly, as if it all had nothing to do with him. "Block letters, stationery without a watermark. It said the writer knew that I had reason to want Moss and Quimper dead and that I had in fact killed them. If I didn't want to have all this divulged, I should leave a sum of money in a remote spot of San Polo. Very good directions were provided."

"Don't tell me that you dropped off the money!" Urbino said with a sinking feeling, but at the same time wondering if he were being taken in. "A large sum, which you got from Barbara. And no, she didn't tell me. The police have been monitoring her financial transactions."

"They'll be peeping into her bedroom next, unless they already have. Yes, I left the money. She had no idea what it was for. I couldn't have Barbara—"

"How convenient to protect her with her own money! If that's what happened!"

A cold fire gleamed in Bobo's eyes.

"I pay my debts in full. I hope you have the same habit." Bobo's voice was quiet, but with an undertone of contempt. "And I *did* leave the money. Call it an error of judgment but I was confused."

"Confused! I would have been furious. Blackmail is despicable. It's only natural to want to strike back!"

"Are you giving me or yourself license? We're not all cut from the same cloth, thank God for that!"

Urbino was astonished at his dislike for the man. It was deeper, stronger, keener than it had ever been.

"You've assumed an air of complacence from the very beginning," Urbino said, hearing the contempt in his own voice. "As if you're far above it all. The threats, the murders, and now what you tell me is blackmail. Start acting in a way that makes sense."

"To who? You?"

Bobo's mouth curved in a superior smile.

"If you're being blackmailed, what's going to happen if you get another demand for money?"

"Ah, but don't you see, my boy? You know everything now, and soon the police will, too."

"Forgive me if I don't believe I know everything! Not about the Helen Creel murder or how Orlando and Livia might fit into the picture. Livia was desperate to talk to you just now. So desperate that she insults Barbara in her own home. Don't count on Barbara's patience for too long! She's not like Rosa, from what I've heard of her. And speaking of Rosa, Orlando said that Moss was very curious about her. I wonder why."

"Do you? And do you also wonder why you've turned into some kind of pathetic voyeur of other peoples' lives, doing damage just for your own pleasure and out of malicious envy and jealousy? Don't *you* count on Barbara's patience for too long! It would have been much better for you to have stayed at Abano and taken care of that toe of yours!"

Bobo's words—all of them—touched Urbino to the quick, but he pulled back from answering him in kind. Instead, in a voice which he tried to make as uncompromising and unruffled as possible, he said: "As for this note you say you received—"

"The note I *received*. Check with Harriet."

"I'm sure an envelope was found but did it really contain a blackmail note? It would be to your advantage to have the police believe it had. A blackmail note that couldn't possibly have originated from Moss and Quimper. And if the envelope did contain a blackmail note, who wrote it? You, the murderer, or someone with strong reason to believe that *you* shot Moss and Quimper? Someone who might even have something that could be considered proof! You say you're not afraid, but I can tell you are—and you should be! Act as much the fool as you want to. Whether it's real or feigned, I don't know. You're a good actor, I give you that. But think about Barbara! You're staying here. You go out together in public. She's in danger simply because of her relationship with you. Violence surrounds you, Bobo. I want to be sure it doesn't touch her in any way and from any direction."

"I'm beginning to think you should confine your sleuthing to things like *this*," the Contessa said to Urbino the next morning on the cemetery island where they had come to see if all the preparations were in place for the bridge of boats at midnight.

The Contessa indicated the moldering ballet slipper on Diaghilev's tomb lying next to a bouquet of irises and a scrap of paper left in memory of Nureyev.

"Always a new—or rather an *old* one. You could crouch by the gate and find out who leaves them! Our curiosity would be

satisfied, and there'd be no danger, no disturbing revelations."
She glanced down at the irises. "Such a shame. Irises die so
quickly." She shivered and drew her coat more tightly against
her throat. She held a bouquet in white chrysanthemums.
"Let's go to the mausoleum."

They walked along the leaf-strewn path. Around them were
graves whose Russian names, the large majority women and
some of them "princesses," evoked the pages of a Tolstoy or
Dostoevsky novel. Urbino often imagined melodramatic lives
and deaths for them, but suspected that the most extraordi-
nary thing about them might be only that they had died in
Venice. The Contessa stared at all the monuments of mortality
and sighed with weariness. Her gait was much slower than
usual, her shoulders drooped.

"My bridge of boats has a cloud over it, doesn't it?

It was starting to get overcast again. But somber weather
would in many ways suit the ceremony. It was a cloud of another kind she meant.

They passed through a gate. Above their heads on both sides
rose *loculi* or burial niches. The walls with their pictures of the
dead bloomed with flowers. As they turned in the direction of
the Da Capo-Zendrini mausoleum, the Contessa said: "If
Alvise were alive, he would want me to stick by Bobo, no matter what!"

It was a comment Urbino knew he shouldn't touch, bristling
as it was with inconsistencies that revealed just how confused
the Contessa was.

"Is that what you're comforting yourself with? From what I
know about Alvise he was nobody's fool."

"And so he wasn't, but he knew what loyalty meant. Bobo's
told me everything and I believe him!

"Everything?"

Yesterday when Urbino and Bobo had finished their talk,
Bobo had said he would speak with the Contessa before going
to the Questura. Urbino had left him to his overdue task

and gone back to the Palazzo Uccello to think things through.

"Yes, *tutto*! All about his argument with Moss in Campo San Luca, the blackmail note, his—his relationship with that poor woman. And if he didn't tell me about her when we were on Torcello—" She caught herself and emphasized: "Yes, everything!"

"I don't think you're a good judge when it comes to Bobo."

"And who are you? Justice blind? Look to the beam in your own eye!"

"But don't you see what it all means? You told him about Helen Creel on Torcello. Not only wasn't he frank with you when he should have been—then, and even much earlier—but he had all that time to consider exactly *what* to tell us, based on what we knew!"

In strained silence they approached the mausoleum with its statues of weeping angels, St. Catherine of Siena, and St. Nicholas of Bari. The statue of St. Nicholas was more weather-eroded than the others and stood less firmly on its base. Nearby was a field of graves in the grim process of being exhumed.

The Contessa took a key from her pocket. Her hand was trembling from a combination of anger and fear. She went up to the iron doors. Lately she had been making an effort to overcome her superstitious dread of the mausoleum, where her name and birthdate had been inscribed during the Conte's lifetime and were waiting for the unknown date.

As she now unlocked the doors and entered the violet interior, she did so with a little frisson and a feeling of claustrophobia. One of her recurring nightmares was being locked behind the stout doors of the mausoleum.

She handed Urbino an empty urn, and he filled it with water from a spigot beside the path. He brought it back to her. She put the chrysanthemums in it, then lit a votive candle and placed it next to the urn on the mauve marble of the altar. She said a prayer, relocked the doors, and came back to Urbino, who was waiting on the path. There was a look of relief on her face, as if she had narrowly escaped an appalling fate.

She glanced at the gaping holes of the graves being exhumed in the near distance, with their piles of dirt, broken pieces of concrete, scattered plastic flowers, and splintered wooden crosses. Without any warning she cried: "They're past caring and past being cared for. But you, *caro*—and us!"

Urbino hardly had time to consider the ambiguity of the Contessa's final pronoun when she said even more portentously: "Look somewhere else for your murderer! If you don't, something frightful is going to happen! You've been led terribly astray and can't even see it. Open your eyes!"

An admonition she herself might heed, Urbino said to himself.

Suddenly they were startled when a loudspeaker summoned the Contessa to the cemetery office for a telephone call. Urbino lingered behind to brood over the graves in the process of exhumation. It was a sight that never failed to depress him. Only the dead whose survivors had long memories and sufficient funds rested in perpetuity. All the others had their bones—or what remained of them—deposited after a meager twelve years' rest in a common grave or in the cemetery's *ossuario*.

He made his way slowly to the cemetery office where the Contessa was waiting.

"That was Corrado." Corrado was a friend attached to the Questura. "I asked him to contact me as soon as he had news about Orlando's autopsy. Mauro told him I was here. Orlando died a natural death! *That* should show you what a house of cards you've been building!"

Insofar as the Contessa could gloat under such circumstances and in such a place, she did so now. But her chin was tilted at too sharp an angle not to tell Urbino that she hoped to convince herself by first convincing him.

As they were about to get into the Contessa's *motoscafo*, they saw Harriet. She was wearing a long dark green raincoat and a knit cap pulled low on her forehead. In her hand was a bouquet of flowers.

"Whatever is *she* doing here!" the Contessa said in an annoyed tone. "She called this morning and said she was still ill. And she has flowers! She doesn't know anyone buried here." She looked at Urbino and said: "Does she?"

"Not as far as I know. There are some things I want to talk to her about. Go on without me."

As the Contessa's *motoscafo* pulled away, she looked through the cabin window with mingled hurt and suspicion.

Harriet, who hadn't noticed the Contessa and Urbino, started when he came up to her, drawing in her receding chin even further. Each time Urbino had seen Harriet in the past two weeks she had looked progressively more weary, even ill. In the sunlight now her face was unhealthily white. The area under her eyes, however, was so dark it looked bruised, but it was her eyes themselves which were most disturbing. They were haunted, frightened, and seemed to look everywhere except at Urbino's own eyes.

"Paying your respects to the dead, Harriet?"

She looked down at her bouquet as if someone had placed it in her hands without her being aware of it.

"Why, yes I am."

"Do you mind if I join you?"

Harriet hesitated for a few seconds, then said: "Of course not."

They went through the gateway with its Gothic carving of St. Michael and the dragon into the cloister. As they walked past the office, Harriet slowed her pace as if she was going to stop, but then continued on through the main gates into the cemetery. Here, however, she stopped. She seemed undecided.

"Where is it that you're going?"

"This way," she said, turning to the left. They walked in silence until they came to a row of graves of infants and children.

"Yes, this is the place."

She went along the walk and looked down at the graves. Most of them had statues and angels and ceramic photographs of the dead infants and children. She stopped in front of a grave with a black-and-white photograph of a little girl in a white bowler hat. The inscription on the cross said: "Mamma Pappa Ti Ricordano 1935–1938."

Harriet propped the bouquet against the stone.

"Her parents are probably not alive anymore to remember her," Harriet said.

This sentimentality was a previously unrevealed quality in Harriet and set Urbino to wondering what other facets she might have that he was unaware of. Of all the suspects, Harriet appeared to have the least motive for having wanted Moss, Quimper, and Gava dead.

She knelt silently for a few minutes until a salamander, one of the many on San Michele, darted in front of her. She jumped to her feet with a sharp cry.

They started to return on the same path they had just come along.

"There are a few things I'd like to ask you, Harriet," Urbino began. "Bobo told me that he received a letter last week. You gave it to him. It didn't go through the mails. Do you remember?"

"Of course I remember!"

Something other than professional pride at remembering details seemed to be behind her vehement response.

"Where did you find it?"

"Under the palazzo door."

"But which one? There are two, not counting the water entrance."

"The door of the palazzo, of course. No, no, what am I saying? Not that door. I mean the door from the *calle.*"

"It would have had to be, wouldn't it, unless the person who left it had been first let through the outside door. Then he—or she—could have easily slipped it under the doors of the palazzo."

Harriet looked confused and frightened. When they reached the cloister, Urbino stopped and put his hand on Harriet's arm.

"You're afraid of Bobo, aren't you, Harriet? You moved out of the Ca' da Capo because you didn't want to be under the same roof with him, didn't you?"

"You're ridiculous! Afraid of him? Of course I'm not! I moved out to have a little privacy!"

"If you're not afraid of Bobo, then who or what are you afraid of? Because you *are* afraid, very afraid. Is it Marco Zeoli?"

Her shrill, high-pitched laugh echoed around the walls of the cloister. Two black-clad women frowned at her. Harriet's unattractive face was now even more pale and pinched. Suddenly she grabbed Urbino's arm and for the first time looked directly into his eyes. There was fear in hers, but also an appeal. He sensed she was about to say something, to ask him for something. Her grip tightened, then weakened.

"Please leave me alone. I beg you!"

She hurried into the church as if seeking refuge.

Urbino went around to the far side of the church and stood on the water-washed steps until a boat had come and gone, then he went back into the cloister. He concealed himself. Harriet was at the cemetery office window. She took a map of the cemetery from a pile and slipped it into her purse.

19

On his walk back to the Palazzo Uccello from the quay across from the cemetery island, Urbino felt close to understanding the twisted sequence of events that had begun when the Contessa had called him back from Marco Zeoli's spa—that had begun, to be more precise, twelve years ago in a therapy room in that same spa where Helen Creel, Hugh Moss's mother, had been murdered. If he hadn't yet been able to piece it all together, it was mainly because of the difficulty of sorting out the lies that were as thick, but far from as salubrious, as the Abano mud in which so many of them had been spawned.

He stared down from a bridge into a canal. Boats desperately in need of paint and repair were tied along the opposite bank. Laundry was strung across the front of a building, its bright colors and geometrical shapes making a contrast with the worn and faded stone. Ivy cascaded down a wall. The water, iridescent with oil, darkly mirrored the scene.

He peered down into its shallow depths. He could make out various forms lurking beneath the surface, teasing him with their distorted appearances. As he knew from low tides and the occasional draining of the canals, they were the most mundane of objects. Umbrellas, carriage wheels, dolls, delivery crates. But hidden as they were beneath the surface they often led to wild imaginings.

He kept looking into the water until he was startled to see his own reflection peering back at him.

Back at the Palazzo Uccello he learned that Gemelli had been trying to get in touch with him.

"It's about Rosa Gava Casarotto-Re," Gemelli said when Urbino called him. "We've talked with the carabinieri in Taormina. She died ten years ago the twenty-ninth of October.

You were right. The same day Gava died. And complete respiratory failure just like Gava. Death by natural cause was the official verdict. But something puzzling to my way of thinking. Why did the woman run out of her medication? Her inhaler was empty and no bottles, empty or otherwise, were found. And no traces of the medication were in her system. Strange, isn't it? And something else. It's about Gava. Something happened to him later the same day."

Before Gemelli told him what it was, Urbino knew. He now remembered something else about Taormina that had been at the back of his mind, something the Contessa had mentioned two weeks ago at Florian's when she was praising Bobo's vigor.

"He almost drowned in the sea," Gemelli said. "Fortunately, Casarotto-Re was with him. Seems as if he's not all bad. He saved Gava from certain death. But what the two men were doing swimming right after the woman's death is beyond me."

"Barbara isn't here," Bobo said to Urbino that afternoon from behind a cloud of smoke. Bobo, Festa, and Peppino were in possession of the *salotto blu*. Bobo, dressed in a stylishly cut tweed suit and looking as if he had recovered completely from his recent indisposition, reclined on the sofa. Festa was standing beneath the Veronese, smoking one of Bobo's Gauloises in a long holder. Peppino dozed on one of the Louis Quinze chairs.

Urbino had the distinct impression that he had interrupted an important discussion.

"She's at the Municipality with Harriet double-checking on the procession tonight," Bobo further clarified, getting up. He looked at Festa. "Perhaps we should go into the garden now. Peppino has been getting a little restless."

Peppino, hearing his name, lifted an eyelid and went back to sleep. Festa picked him up.

"I'm afraid it looks like rain," Urbino said.

"We won't melt!" Festa said coldly. "Let's go, Bobo."

"Rain!" Bobo said enthusiastically. "That will be marvelous for the procession. How atmospheric!" He recited an appropriate quotation from D'Annunzio about inclement weather, then said: "Indulge in whatever you like, Urbino." He indicated the low table crowded with covered dishes, plates, two champagne glasses, and a bottle of Dom Pérignon. "There's only a swallow of champagne left, I'm afraid, but just as well, I suppose, with that troublesome toe of yours. Barbara said she won't be back until six. I don't know if you want to hang around that long."

When Bobo and Festa had gone, Urbino uncovered a few of the dishes, discovering some of the choicest morsels from the Ca' da Capo-Zendrini kitchen and larder. He spread some beluga caviar on a cracker and washed it down with the remnants of the Dom Pérignon.

He looked through the window of the *salotto* into the garden where he saw Bobo and Festa walking slowly past the stone lions. He slipped up to the next floor and went into Bobo's room. Urbino, who had stayed in the room on numerous occasions himself, noticed a new addition on the wall: a portrait of the Contessa reclining against Tunisian cushions. It had formerly hung in the library.

What he hoped to find in Bobo's room he didn't know. Something. Anything. The police had already gone through the room, and in any case Bobo was too sly a man to leave anything incriminating around. He would either have it on his person or would have destroyed it.

A leather address book lay on the night table. It was of fine Florentine design, similar to the one he had seen in Gava's hotel suite. He looked through it. The police must have made a copy of its contents. The Moss and Creel names didn't appear, nor was there an entry for Marco Zeoli or John Flint, although there was one for Oriana. The nib of a fountain pen had made a neat black line through Orlando's name. Festa had obviously changed her address many times, for addresses were crossed out and new ones put in so often that Bobo had had to move to the back of the book. All the earlier entries had been under "L." Harriet's address in the ghetto was entered.

A footstep sounded in the hall. He put the address book down. He hadn't thought through what he would do or say if Bobo caught him. But the footsteps passed. Most likely Mauro or Lucia. Urbino breathed more easily and continued his search.

There were numerous volumes of D'Annunzio's and Bobo's own books. A large envelope was stuffed with reviews of Bobo's performances and books and publicity clippings, with photographs that showed how little he had changed over the past fifteen years. One clipping was of the demonstration in Milan several years ago that Bobo had mentioned: FEMINISTS DELAY D'ANNUNZIO PERFORMANCE. The account held nothing of significance.

Piled up beneath one of the ceramic palm trees were several video cassettes of Bobo's performances, one of them of the opening night of *Pomegranate* at the Teatro del Ridotto. Urbino became increasingly nervous that Bobo and Festa would return from the garden and he started to hurry. Rings and cuff links sparkled at him from a small coffer, designer suits and jackets and shirts in the armoire wafted Bobo's scent at Urbino, a combination of expensive cologne and cigarettes; socks, underwear, and shirts displayed their neat folds from the Florentine-papered drawers. Pairs upon pairs of shoes on trees were arranged in a row in a corner. The laundry hamper was empty.

No diary, no money, no passport or identity papers, no letters, no postcards. He was about to leave when he thought of something. Bobo's toiletry kit. He found it on the shelf in the armoire. Sleeping pills, sedatives, throat lozenges—what seemed to be a gross of these—scissors, nail clippers. Then, beneath the other things, was something that gave him considerable pleasure if not the enlightenment he was seeking. It was a tube of paste used to affix dentures more firmly.

He didn't want to risk looking through Bobo's bathroom. He was already pressing his luck. He slipped out of the room and down the hall.

Harriet's former room was obviously still in the process of being cleaned. The window was open, the shutters thrown back. The furnishings were simple and tasteful, having been collected from other rooms to suit Harriet's unpretentious taste. The most unusual piece was an Empire escritoire that used to be in the morning room. Its drawers and pigeonholes held nothing. The blotter was slightly soiled, but there were no doodles or mysterious lines of script that might be conveniently held up to a mirror to spell out the incriminating name or number.

The armoire was empty except for hangers. The bookshelf contained nothing but a map of Venice that could be bought at any kiosk in the city. He unfolded it. The Ca' da Capo-Zendrini on the Grand Canal was marked with a neat "X" as were the Palazzo Uccello and what Urbino realized was Marco Zeoli's apartment. He refolded the map and put it back.

Regretting that he hadn't looked through Harriet's room immediately after she had moved out, he went to the open window and peered out from behind the curtains. The garden was below. Urbino searched in vain for any sign of Bobo and Festa on the paths or among the boxwood and laurel.

He was about to go back downstairs when he heard Festa's voice floating up to him as clear and distinct as a bell. They must have been in the pergola, one of the few concealed spots in the garden. The fact that Festa's voice, then Bobo's quick response, came so distinctly was not a result of their loudness—for they were in fact quite low—but of the peculiar acoustics of the Contessa's garden, something Urbino had noted before but forgotten. The couple's voices soon faded away, but he had heard enough. It set him to thinking of the night of the Contessa's gala, the night Orlando had fallen ill. Bobo and Festa emerged from the pergola and started to walk back to the palazzo, still engaged in what seemed to be intimate conversation, which he could no longer hear.

Urbino turned quickly from the window and bumped with considerable force into a corner of the armoire. It was proof of the force with which he hit it that not only did he get an excruciating pain in his shoulder but that the armoire shifted ever so slightly. And when it did, he heard a rush of sound as of something slipping and sliding. The sound, which came from behind the armoire, moved to the floor and stopped. He rubbed his shoulder and looked behind the armoire. A small space was visible where it didn't quite meet the wall, a space that his collision had obviously made wider. He looked down at the floor behind the armoire and saw a thin, dark rectangular object. His hand was too large to fit in the space. He pushed the armoire farther from the wall so that he could put his hand in. It touched and then grasped paper.

He withdrew the object. It was a large envelope not at all unlike the one he had just found in Bobo's room. Inside were what he had found in Bobo's envelope. Clippings. And each of them was autographed with an intimacy. If the clippings had shown naked men and women instead of ones fashionably dressed, they couldn't have been more revealing.

Things slotted into place. He folded the envelope of clippings and stuffed them in the inside pocket of his jacket.

He hurried from the Ca' da Capo-Zendrini before Bobo and Festa could see him. He had to call Gemelli.

PART FOUR

The Isle of the Dead

1

Everyone had been provided with votive candles or lamps. Urbino turned around to look behind him when he was halfway across the bridge. A string of lights snaked back to Venice. The city itself lay dark and sleeping beneath a low sky. The weather had become overcast, but the night had turned warm, sending fog drifting in from the lagoon.

Ahead of him the Contessa, dressed in black with silver trim, was helped by Bobo over the pontoon bridge. Her step was firm, but careful, and she held her candle in front of her, although lanterns illuminated the way.

How many of this small procession really wanted to be there? To judge by their expressions and the way they plodded along, certainly not the priest who had officiated at midnight mass at the nearby Church of the Gesuiti or the scattering of city officials.

Festa, sans Peppino, had the air of someone suffering through it all only for the pleasure it gave to rivet her kohl-rimmed eyes at the Contessa's and Bobo's backs in anticipation of a misstep by one or both of them.

Oriana had begged off, but Flint was there with a bouquet of violets for her parents' grave pressed against his dark velvet jacket. His countenence was suitably solemn as if he expected his picture to be taken at any moment.

Zeoli, his long face in a scowl, stepped over the planks with the caution of a man who knew from professional experience the indignities caused by injured limbs. Harriet, whom he occasionally helped to make her timid way, was so be-scarfed, be-hatted, and be-gloved that she was barely recognizable except for the fearful eyes that contemplated the invading fog as if it were a pestilential vapor.

The only people, other than the Contessa, who seemed to be in the spirit of things were half a dozen hobbling women in widow's weeds who clearly preferred the damp and the fog to sleepless hours in front of their heaters.

And so they all slowly made their way to the island of the dead, whose brick walls, cypresses, and coffin runway, wreathed with fog, were barely visible in the near distance.

2

The procession, stately when it had crept across the bridge of boats, scattered soon after reaching the island. The officials, after enduring the priest's benediction, were now slipping out of the church to their waiting boats. The widows, for whom the fog and darkness presented little problem given their familiarity with the cemetery, moved off in a flock with their flowers and spades and lamps.

"Urbino," Bobo whispered, "I must talk with you. Join Father Vida and me in the Cappella Emiliana. Excuse us, Barbara."

Bobo drew Father Vida into the chapel and started to speak to him enthusiastically. When Urbino joined them, Bobo turned to him and said in English: "I'll speak quickly. I'm sure we're being observed. No, don't look around. Our good priest here doesn't understand a scrap of English, but I'll throw out some words about the chapel to confuse him or whoever else might be listening. I got another blackmail note! Mauro found it in the little courtyard by the outside door an hour ago when someone rang the bell. I haven't told Barbara. *Gugliemo dei Grigi!*" he threw in, naming the artist who had designed the chapel. The Contessa glanced at them nervously from where she was standing with Harriet and Zeoli. "And no, I haven't even had a chance to tell the police—*1530! Tutto marmo!* A map of the cemetery was attached. I'm to go to a place marked on it. Somewhere on the other side. The grave of the Baron Corvo. I assume it's supposed to be ironic or something, since Rolfe gave himself the name and title. *Ruskin!* Leave us here in the chapel and don't attract any attention, but follow me to the grave. Do you know where it is? *Gotica!*"

Urbino said he did. He remembered that both Festa and Flint had displayed a knowledge of the Baron Corvo on separate occasions. He left Bobo and the bewildered, faintly smiling priest to join Flint. The former model was looking down at a map of the cemetery, the one given out at the cemetery office.

"Can you help me, Urbino? Oriana marked her family's tomb but I'm still confused. Could you give me my bearings so I can bring these there?"

He indicated the demure bouquet of violets. Urbino explained the best way to get to the tomb. It wasn't far from the Da Capo-Zendrini mausoleum. To get his own bearings Urbino's eye strayed to the other corner of the map where the Baron Corvo was buried.

"Thank you! I'd better go right away. I don't want to miss the boats returning to Venice. A cemetery isn't my idea of a place to spend the night!"

"Mine either!" Festa said from a nearby pew. She threw an angry glance at Bobo, who was still talking with the priest. Flint excused himself and left. Fog curled into the church from the briefly opened door.

"I've told Bobo and I'm telling you," Festa went on. "You can tell *her* if you want!" There was no need for the irritated nod in the Contessa's direction for Urbino to know whom she meant. "I'm sitting right here until the boats go back so don't forget me! I don't know why I came!"

"Why did you?"

She pressed her plump lips together and frowned. Urbino excused himself and joined the Contessa, who was moving slowly toward the door with Harriet and Zeoli.

"Harriet and I are going to the mausoleum. Why don't you come with us? Marco was going to come, but he's feeling ill." The man in fact didn't look at all well. His eyes were bloodshot and his sallow skin had a sickly shine. "You should rest here, Marco dear. Maybe you can keep Livia company. I think she'll be on the first boat back." She cast an amused glance over at Festa, who was rummaging through her large pocketbook. "So will you join us, Urbino? Bobo says he has his own respects to pay. Where, I don't know. He's being mysterious."

"Why don't you and Harriet go on ahead, but if you don't mind, give me about twenty minutes before you leave the church. I'd like to go to Pound's grave first."

"That fascist!"

"Don't let the Barone hear you say that," Zeoli said with a sickly grin. "D'Annunzio had his sympathies with Il Duce, too."

"No more of your criticisms of D'Annunzio tonight, Marco," the Contessa said. "You should have heard him, Urbino. Filling poor Harriet's ears with all sorts of terrible stories. Now, you just sit right there next to Livia, Marco. You take good care of him, Livia. I'm sure you must have a whole pharmacy of medicines in that big bag. You doctor him up if he needs it. As you wish, Urbino. If you must go to that ghastly man's grave, do it. You know where the mausoleum is. We'll give you your twenty minutes."

Very little of this interchange seemed to register on Harriet, who had a preoccupied look on her plain face.

Urbino hurried through the door and into the fog-filled cloister, then into a crypt on the other side of the cloister where Gemelli had said Urbino's contact would be. Urbino informed him about what he was going to do and what Bobo had told him about the newest blackmail note and the Baron Corvo's grave. He made sure the police officer knew exactly where Corvo's grave and the Da Capo-Zendrini mausoleum were.

Then he went into the cemetery.

Fog swirled around him and invaded his clothes. What little he was able to see gleamed as if lit by an unearthly light. Sounds, all of them muted and most of them indistinguishable, fell dully upon his ears like some manifestation of the fog. The only sounds he could identify were the scratching of what were either the cemetery's ubiquitous rats or the salamanders that had frightened Harriet, and the periodic bleat of a foghorn out in the lagoon.

He proceeded a short distance along the wall to the left of the entrance, then stopped. He pressed himself up closely against one of the tombs built into the wall. He had only to wait a few minutes. Footsteps sounded from the cloister, paused briefly at the entrance to the cemetery, then turned right without any perceptible hesitation. They continued in the general direction of the Baron Corvo's grave before being swallowed up in the thick air.

Try though he did, Urbino couldn't make out any form, nor could he identify the footsteps as belonging to a man or a woman.

He went onto the same path the footsteps had taken. He advanced slowly because of the fog and because he wanted to make as little sound as possible on the gravel. Old-fashioned lanterns placed close to the ground provided only minimal illumination, so that someone could have been within touching distance without being seen. Occasionally he thought he saw the glimmer of a lamp and heard a voice, but the fog and the dark deceived as well as concealed. If he hadn't taken this path so often, he would have had to feel his way even more than he was.

Yet he didn't catch up with whomever was ahead. If he could only see who it was, it would be enough. If it was Bobo, his mind would be more at ease, for the man couldn't be in two places. Then he could be almost assured that Bobo had told him the truth about the blackmail note. So much depended on this, for this last blackmail note had been an unforeseen development that might ruin everything. If he had been wrong about the realizations he had come to in Harriet's former room—

But he didn't allow himself to reconsider. He had to be right. He continued to crawl through the fog, calculating how much more time he had before the Contessa and Harriet started out from the church.

The grave of the Baron Corvo, who had taken part in a similar procession to the cemetery at the turn of the century, was farther to the right near the surrounding wall. Urbino continued along with the slight help of the lanterns, but mainly by instinct and habit. Occasionally the fog lifted to reveal more of the path ahead, a water spigot with a pail, or one or two grave markers. Most of the latter were cheap wooden crosses about three feet high with ceramic photographs or plastic-covered snapshots of the dead. The name of the dead was painted crudely on the horizontal bar of the cross, sometimes without any dates.

He made good progress and was soon in an area of burial niches built in tiers near the outer wall of the cemetery. He stopped behind a column near the water gate. Globes on top of the wall cast their meager light down on the scene. The Baron Corvo's niche was on the topmost tier and faced the lagoon and the sleeping city. A movable metal stairway nearby provided access to the higher graves. Broken pieces of marble, large rocks, discarded crosses, urns, and grave markers with photographs littered the area.

Before the fog drifted in from the lagoon again, Urbino made out a tall figure standing beneath the skeleton stairway. It was Bobo. His cigarette glowed brightly and then dimmed. Urbino was tempted to stay longer, but he now knew that

Bobo, who hadn't seen him, was where he had said he would be. Somewhere nearby were policemen. They would have to handle whoever might show up to meet Bobo.

As for Urbino, he had to get to the Da Capo-Zendrini mausoleum as quickly as possible now.

Still not sure, however, that he wasn't being tricked in some way that took advantage of his blind spot about Bobo, he started to retrace his way with a sense of urgency.

Surely those were footsteps behind him. He stopped, but heard only the fog horn moaning. A few seconds later a blow smashed against the back of his head. He dropped to his knees. He looked up and saw a figure looming above him. He put his hand up to avoid the next blow.

The Contessa and Harriet groped along the path, using the feeble illumination of the lanterns as their only guide. At the insistence of Harriet, who seemed anxious to get away from Festa and Zeoli after everyone else had left the church, the Contessa had shaved five minutes off the twenty she had promised Urbino to wait before leaving.

The fog was one of the thickest the Contessa had ever had the misfortune to be out in. So absorbed was she in what Harriet was saying that it was a wonder the Contessa didn't fall flat on her face.

"Don't you see, Barbara? He abandoned Helen Creel when he found out that she had no real money—that it was all her son's, because of her father's will! I know you love him but love can do terrible things. I've been driven mad!"

Harriet grabbed the Contessa's hand and moved a step ahead of her, as if she were urging the Contessa to the mausoleum, afraid she might now turn back. The Contessa suddenly wished that she had waited those extra five minutes. She desperately wanted Urbino to be at the mausoleum waiting for them. Whyever did he have to go to Pound's grave?

The mausoleum rose up in her mind with its cold marble walls and its eroding statues, with her name and birthdate engraved and waiting. How could she ever have thought that she had banished her dread of the place?

"Moss never forgot Bobo's face," Harriet was saying, her breathing shallow and wheezy, her voice seeming to come from a long way off. "You know how little he's changed in the past ten years. As handsome as ever. My mother always told me to run as fast as I could from handsome men. As if I ever had to do the running!"

Harriet broke out into her loud, hysterical laugh, but cut it off as if with a knife and clapped one hand over her mouth, with the other pulling the Contessa along.

The Contessa peered into the fog. She could see only vague shapes—peculiar flickering lights, mausoleums, grave markers, trees, unmoving forms that looked like men and women but certainly must be statues. Perhaps Urbino was somewhere nearby on the path ahead or behind them. She thought she heard a footfall.

"Urbino? Is that you?"

Her voice was swallowed by the fog.

"We've both been fools, Barbara. But I've been the bigger one. I—"

The Contessa felt as if the fog had crept into her mind, confusing it, and into her heart, giving it a mortal chill. She started to lose track of what Harriet was saying.

"—and he said that all we needed was money, that we already had love, and I believed him. And when I told him what I heard Moss and Quimper say in the garden the night of your reception, that was all he needed to get his mind going. I'm so sorry for what I've done to you, Barbara." She gripped the Contessa's arm more tightly and the Contessa started to pull away. "I never thought he was the one who killed them! And now I think he knows that I know! Oh, my God, what was that?"

Both women froze. Harriet's nails dug into the Contessa's flesh.

"Let's hurry," the Contessa said. "We can't be far from the mausoleum. I have the key."

As they hurried along, the Contessa gave a shudder at the thought of seeking safety behind the heavy doors of the mausoleum.

His watch was smashed. Slowly, painfully, he got to his feet. How long had he been unconscious? One minute? Ten minutes? Longer?

He touched his head. His hand came away sticky. He smelled his own blood.

He stifled a call for help. Whoever had hit him hoped he was dead or at least unconscious. Better to leave it that way, better to stay off the paths. Moving with the slowness of a nightmare, never sure if his legs weren't going to buckle, he struck out across the field of graves.

As long as he walked in a straight line between the graves he was fine, but he occasionally lost his sense of direction from the effects of the blow and the fog. He bumped into grave markers, flower urns, and concrete planters. The unmistakable squeal and scratching of rats assaulted his ears. They ran across his feet and plopped down from the grave markers. He both cursed and was grateful for the fog and darkness that hid how alive the field must be with them. He tripped and fell onto the damp, yeasty earth. He scrambled up as quickly as he could but not quickly enough. A rat grazed the top of his head. Shuddering, wondering if the blood was attracting them, he continued to creep along.

His eye was caught by scattered, flickering lights that burned through the fog. These weren't votive candles or lamps. They were the *fuochi fatui*, fires fueled by gases from the decomposing bodies buried close to the surface. The coldness of their burning mocked him with what it seemed to say about the illumination the living might expect of the dead.

At one point he thought he had lost his way, had become turned around and might be going back toward the Baron Corvo's grave or deeper into the cemetery. But the fog lifted and thinned to reveal a row of graves whose names he remembered recording in his journal for possible research. Yes, he was still moving in the right direction. He crossed a path and entered another field. He was only a short distance from the Da Capo-Zendrini mausoleum.

He should have been warned by the rubble that he knocked against and stepped on, that sometimes crunched beneath his feet or obstructed his way. Realization came a second too late as he tripped and fell into a shallow excavation filled with water. It was a disinterred grave. He now remembered seeing the graves in the process of being disinterred when he was here with the Contessa.

He scrambled up the muddy side of the grave. A woman screamed. He pulled himself out and grabbed a large piece of concrete. He ran toward the mausoleum. A sharp crack cut the air.

"Oh, my God!" came a voice he immediately recognized as the Contessa's.

The crack came again, followed by the grate and bang of a metal door closing.

Fog wreathed the mausoleum. A votive candle on the steps shimmered and quickened the faces of the two stone saints. Urbino rushed up behind a figure with a gun, who was frantically searching the ground. Other figures ran in their direction from the fog. Urbino brought the concrete down heavily on the man's head.

Flint dropped the gun and staggered toward the steps of the mausoleum. He grasped the statue of St. Nicholas with both arms and slowly started to fall backward. The saint, dislodged, came down massively on top of him.

From behind the closed doors of the mausoleum came the Contessa's terrified, muffled screams.

Death in the Salon

"Couldn't you have found the key more quickly!" the Contessa reprimanded Urbino for what must have been the fifth time since they had sat down in the Chinese salon. "I was absolutely frantic!"

Urbino remembered only too well the dazed look on her face when he had finally been able to turn the lock of the mausoleum doors. Her hands, her dress, even her face were smeared with Harriet's blood.

The Contessa took a deep breath that seemed to savor a great deal: the deep repose of the salon, the smoke-free air, her near escape from death, and perhaps even the second plate of petits fours in front of her. She picked one up now, its pink frosting setting off the dove of her dress.

She noticed Urbino's gaze and said: "Food is life, *caro*, and I intend to live!"

The chin she tilted at him showed a slight weight gain. She had remained secluded at the Ca' da Capo-Zendrini for the past week, refusing to return phone calls or to see anyone except the police—and that only under sufferance. But today she had called him, saying: "It's time to face the world."

There wasn't much of the world to face this afternoon, however, except each other and some unanswered questions, some pieces that each needed to put together for not only their edification, but their comfort as well.

With the air of clearing the table so that they could begin, the Contessa said: "I've sent Bobo packing."

But Bobo had gone only as far as the Gritti Palace. His presence was required for a while longer in Venice.

"I've had the *salotto blu* and the room upstairs disinfected of his abominable smoke, and every single solitary volume of D'Annunzio is packed away!"

There were more subtle changes that she didn't mention, among them a return to her old, familiar scent and less sunshine in her hair.

"It won't be as easy to get rid of his memory," Urbino said gently, now able to be more considerate of her feelings than he had been recently.

"I'm a stronger woman than you think, *caro*! And all the stronger for having been so weak. But I don't *want* to forget! Not any of it! Not what he did to Helen Creel! Not what he wanted to do to that poor couple! Oh, he might not have killed them, but he wanted them dead! And I certainly have no intention of forgetting what he was doing to me! His and everyone else's golden goose!"

The Contessa's image was certainly appropriate, not only because of all the ruffled feathers she was now displaying but because of one of the many things Harriet had told her about Flint. He had asked Harriet, from her privileged position as the Contessa's live-in secretary, to be on the lookout for anything about the Contessa or Urbino that could be turned into money. Then, when Bobo's secret fell into his lap, Flint schemed to have the Contessa pay, unwittingly, for the keeping of that secret, perhaps forever.

The Contessa closed her eyes and rubbed her temples. Surely she was also thinking of what Bobo might have ended up doing to secure as much of her money for himself as he could. She looked at Urbino and, straining for a tone of normalcy, said: "So tell me, *caro*, how was it that you finally realized it was Flint?"

Urbino knew that the Contessa wanted—she needed—to have her mind focused on the facts, on what had really happened, so that she could begin to heal. It would make little difference to her if he—or she herself—repeated things they both already knew. They needed to do this together. Urbino was more than willing, but he was afraid of one or two aspects that might have to surface.

"It was partly thanks to the acoustics of your garden," he began, knowing that this area held no dangers. "Before the procession I was at the window of Harriet's former room and heard Bobo and Livia's conversation in the pergola as clear as anything, even though they were talking softly. It wasn't *what* they were saying but the fact that I could hear them so well. I suddenly realized that Harriet could have overheard whatever Moss and Quimper were talking about the night of your reception when she went up to her room to get one of Bobo's publicity photographs. I figured that there was a good chance they were talking about Bobo and Helen Creel.

"Right after turning from the window I discovered the envelope with pages torn from fashion magazines. All of them were fashion layouts in which Flint figured, and he had signed each one. I didn't piece together anything like the whole picture, of course, but it struck me that the two of them could have conspired to blackmail Bobo and that somehow they were responsible for Moss's and Quimper's murders. I was already leaning toward Flint because he had had the most contact with the couple and was desperate for money. As for Harriet, she didn't have an alibi for the time Moss and Quimper were murdered."

"Because she was walking around in a daze after leaving Marco's!" Obviously, whatever Harriet had done to harm the Contessa had been forgiven and would have been even if the woman hadn't died in her arms. "She wasn't comfortable with the idea of blackmail, and she never would have gone along with anything like murder! She thought for so long that—that Bobo had killed Moss and Quimper. Flint told her that he had set up a meeting with the couple while she was at Marco's to work out an even better plan to blackmail Bobo and that, after he left them, Bobo killed them."

"Flint was determined to convince them that night—one way or another—not to tell you about Helen Creel. Once you knew about her, once you knew the kind of man Bobo was, Flint lost his power over him because he knew Bobo would do almost anything to keep you in the dark. Moss and Quimper were in a perfect position to make a lot of money for them all, but they refused. Moss wanted revenge—to ruin everything between you and Bobo, for the way Bobo had destroyed his family. So Flint murdered them."

"I don't know why the Substitute Prosecutor can't make a case against him for murdering them!"

"What Harriet told you is hearsay."

"It's the truth! All of it practically her dying words! Unless it's *my* word that's in doubt!"

"You know how these things work. Unless someone saw him do it or he confesses, he won't be charged with their murders."

"But he killed her because she knew he was the murderer—and tried to do the same to me!"

"Her murder may be the only thing he'll be prosecuted for. Thank God, they found most of the money in his room. But what isn't hearsay is speculation."

"What about Orlando then? Isn't there any way it can be proved that Flint killed him?"

"Flint didn't kill Orlando."

"He didn't? Who did then?"

There was panic in her eyes. She was afraid of the answer. He didn't keep her in suspense.

"No one."

"No one? But I don't understand."

"He seems to have committed suicide."

" 'Seems to'? Don't play with me!"

"But I'm afraid I can't do any better than that—and neither can the police. Flint definitely didn't kill him though. Although Oriana admits she lied about Flint being with her the night of the murder—he convinced her he'd be needlessly hassled if she didn't—she swears they were together when Orlando died."

"Someone else could have emptied his pills into the toilet and thrown his inhaler out the window and not even been there when he had his attack."

"If someone had done that," Urbino said, "he would have had to be pretty sure not only that Orlando was going to have an attack but also that it would be severe enough to bring about his death. Only one person could have been so sure—and also thrown away the pills and the inhaler. Orlando himself. It's completely possible he induced his attack. When I visited him, he mentioned some of the things in the suite that could trigger one. Dust, tobacco smoke, and newsprint."

"And he was found grasping newspaper!"

"The newspaper, or one of the other things, or a combination of them, probably brought on the attack—by his own intention. Who knows? He might even have wanted it to look like murder—to make some people uneasy. I'm sure that he didn't want to live. Obsessed as he was with his sister's death—and suffering from the same illness—he probably found a grim appropriateness in dying on the same day. And he tried to kill himself at least one time before that we know about."

"When Bobo saved him from drowning at Taormina!"

"Exactly."

What he didn't voice about Bobo's act of bravery was that it might have been less to save his brother-in-law's life than to give himself a chance to get his hands on the money Rosa had left her brother. If Orlando had died then, none of his money would have gone to Bobo. Bobo had needed time to work on him, but his efforts had failed. The closest he had come to Orlando's money was through Livia.

"It will make me feel better if I just get it straight in my head what was going on the night of the murders," the Contessa said. "You must have figured it out by now."

"With the help of what we know for sure and what seems probable. We know from Bobo that Moss was going to tell you everything, that he was finished toying with him with things like the accusations. Moss was probably no longer getting satisfaction from only making Bobo dread being exposed. Bobo called him and Quimper on the Flora house phone and said he wanted to meet them. An attempt to dissuade Moss from his plan. They walked together, Bobo and Moss argued in Campo San Luca, and then the couple must have gone to see Flint, probably at his apartment, while Bobo and Harriet were on their separate walks. Moss told Flint they were definitely not going to blackmail Bobo through you. Given the time involved, Moss must have called you from Flint's phone to show him he meant what he was saying. Flint, seeing his scheme falling apart, tracked them to the Erberia on their way to see you, and shot them. From first insinuating himself into their plan of revenge against Bobo, with Harriet as the essential liaison between them all and you, Flint made sure that the whole game became his. And then he played it just the way he wanted. He—"

"I can't tell you how good it makes me feel to see that you've thrown yourself back into the fray, Barbara," interrupted a woman's deep voice.

The Contessa and Urbino had been so absorbed that they hadn't noticed the approach of the speaker. It was Oriana, dressed in black and purple. With her was her husband, Filippo.

"We can't punish ourselves forever for having made a mistake. Filippo understands, don't you, dear? *He*'s made quite a few in his time! And I'm sure Urbino understands."

"Why don't you join us?" Urbino said.

"We wouldn't think of it! You two need to be alone together for a long, long time. We're off to a Vivaldi concert. But we thought we'd stop by to say hello when we saw you in here. Give me a call, Barbara. We've got a lot to talk about."

Filippo, whose only reaction to all this had been a benign, if slightly strained expression, smiled his good will as the two of them left the salon.

"Well, she's certainly bounced back!" the Contessa said, staring after the departing couple. "I wish I had her resilience!"

"Is that what you call it? She'll be on the prowl again before too long."

The Contessa pretended not to hear him and went on: "She gives me encouragement. No matter what I've been through, at least it's not as bad as what she has. Maybe I'll be able to start feeling that everything isn't my fault."

"Your fault?"

"If I were a beggar maid—or a beggar *matron*—there would have been no money to tempt any of them, is what I mean. Not Harriet. Not Flint. Not anyone!" She went on in a calmer voice, staring out into Piazza San Marco: "When I was just a girl at St. Brigid's, I believed there were answers to everything—unless they were the Mysteries of the Church," she added with a little laugh. "But I've learned that there aren't. It's a delusion. A trap." She started and her eyes widened. "Well, I never! Can you believe this!"

What the Contessa meant was evident as soon as Urbino looked out into the Piazza. Bobo and Livia Festa were hurrying across the square under the same umbrella. Peppino, pressed against Festa's ample breasts, was wearing an emerald-green rain jacket that matched his mistress's. They stopped when they reached the arcade in front of the Chinese salon and Bobo folded the umbrella. Festa was the first to see the Contessa and Urbino. She nodded, poker-faced. Bobo shot them a twisted smile, then grabbed Festa's elbow and hurried her toward the entrance of Florian's.

"So brazen!" the Contessa said, as if both of them had been parading stark naked through the square. "But they wouldn't dare come in here now that they've seen us!"

They did, however, going through the passageway behind the Chinese salon to one of the larger rooms. Neither Bobo nor Festa looked in their direction, but Peppino stared into the salon with an almost human curiosity.

"I have something to tell you about Livia," Urbino said.

"I hope her fat ears burn like fire!"

"They very well might. It's about Orlando's will—his *other* will," Urbino emphasized.

"Another one besides the one he left Livia all that money in?"

"Made out shortly after he came here. He added Livia's share to his original bequest to the medical school. The will was witnessed by two employees of the Flora who didn't mention it until the day before your procession. Livia must have found it and destroyed it. Maybe the morning she discovered his body. She called his room first. There was no answer. She must have assumed he was out and let herself in with the key she had made. Certainly Orlando never gave her one. She probably searched his room from time to time. She couldn't help but have noticed that Orlando didn't think of her in the same way anymore. He might even have taunted her with having drawn up a new will recently. I think he had just found out something about her that turned him against her completely. Maybe he hired a private detective. His address book was missing. She must have taken it so that when the police went through it they wouldn't find the name of this detective—and been led back to her. She destroyed the new will and the address book. We'll never find them—but what she didn't think about was that Orlando sent a certified copy of the new will to his *avvocato* in Rome. She's smart, but not as smart as she thinks."

The Contessa was trying to recall something. Her brow was slightly furrowed.

"I think I know what happened to the will and the address book. Livia and Bobo burned them in the fireplace of the *salotto blu* the day after Orlando died. I noticed there had been a fire."

"So did I that same day. When I was in the *salotto*, Harriet came in and looked in the fireplace, too. She might have known the two of them were burning something. It probably only served to feed her fear of Bobo."

"What might Orlando have learned about Livia?"

"If a private detective was involved and we can locate him, we'll have a definite answer. My guess is that it had something to do with Rosa. The money was originally willed to Livia because of her kindness to Rosa. Orlando conducted much of his life based on his feelings for his sister. Yes, it must have had something to do with Rosa."

He tried to gauge whether the Contessa suspected the drift of his comments. He could read nothing in her face.

"Livia was in Taormina when Rosa died," he went on. "Rosa died ten years ago on the twenty-ninth of October. She had an attack, she was alone, she had run out of medicine for her inhaler. Orlando, Livia, and Bobo were all out having dinner at the Granduca. They—"

"Stop right there! I won't hear another syllable!"

Several customers looked over at her.

"I don't care if Livia and Bobo hear me in the next room! I won't have you insinuate such things. You're determined to make Bobo guilty of even more than he is! I won't have it!" Her face crumpled and she started to cry. "How much more can one person bear! I regret nothing, I tell you. I felt something. Is there anything to be ashamed of in that? Is there?"

He reached out and held her hand.

"I'm sorry. I didn't want to upset you."

"You did! You're trying to plant it in my mind that Rosa's death wasn't all that it appeared to be. And I won't take as an excuse that you feel I must face the truth, whatever that means! Haven't I had to contort myself like somebody made out of india rubber to save *you* from knowing the truth at times? Excuse me. I'm going to the lounge."

She picked up her purse and left the salon. Urbino had more than ten minutes to consider her words and his own intentions. Perhaps he should have kept his suspicions about Rosa's death to himself. The Contessa, as she had told him, had already "sent Bobo packing." What had he hoped to accomplish by telling her what he had? Had she been right? Was he paying her back for showing him, through her feeling for Bobo, that something was missing from his own life? Or had he been discouraging any future contacts with Bobo, once her hurt had dulled and she might begin to rationalize his behavior? Whatever it was, he wasn't pleased with himself. Of one thing he was sure: He hadn't always acted well with the most important person in his life. He made a firm purpose of amendment about himself and his relationship with the Contessa.

He was thus in a penitent mood when she returned, looking surprisingly composed. She gave him a tremulous smile as she slipped into the banquette.

"I've just had the indescribable pleasure of sharing a mirror with Livia—or perhaps I should describe it as having my reflection crowded out by hers! Chattering on about her and Bobo's plans for the New Year! She's putting a brave face on it after having lost her slice of Orlando's money."

"From what Gemelli said I don't think she knows yet."

"Doesn't know yet! Then Bobo doesn't either! How marvelous!"

She looked at him with much of her old vivacity. The moments they had just been apart had not only made him more penitent but her more forgiving, as she now made clear when she said: "I know that you always have my best interests at heart, *caro*. I trust you. I just wish sometimes that you would trust yourself more."

He was trying to decipher this somewhat cryptic comment when she quickly went on: "Maybe you think I've been a fool. But I never felt that way and I still don't! I'd rather misplace my affections a hundred times instead of not taking a chance. Oh, passion comes in strange forms, *caro*. It has nothing to do with what we expect. I've seen a bit more of life than you. You're still young. It isn't too late! It's never too late!"

He almost expected her to reach out and grasp his arm in her urgency, but instead she took a petit four crowned with a házelnut and bit into it. They sat in silence, each lost in his own thoughts, until the Contessa said: "By the way, have you felt any twinges lately?"

For a moment he didn't know what she meant.

"Oh, my toe. It's been fine. I'd forgotten about it."

"All you needed was something to take you out of yourself. But just listen to me! We certainly don't want any more murders, do we? Besides, you have me again."

"As we were?"

"I certainly hope not! A woman needs more than that!"